GARLIC & GAULOISES

HEMMIE MARTIN

Winter Goose
PUBLISHING
where words take flight

Winter Goose Publishing
45 Lafayette Road #114
North Hampton, CA 03862

www.wintergoosepublishing.com
Contact Information: info@wintergoosepublishing.com

GARLIC & GAULOISES

COPYRIGHT © 2015 Hemmie Martin

First Edition, November 2015

Cover Art by Winter Goose Publishing
Typesetting by Odyssey Books

ISBN: 978-1-941058-37-4

Published in the United States of America

To Jessica Violet, with love
Happy 21st Birthday

Chapter 1

Teardrops of rain inched down the leaded windows, reflecting Alice's mood perfectly. The heavy silence in the sparsely decorated crematorium chapel was only broken by her blowing her nose; the two other guests had shuffled off to a coffee morning at the local community centre.

"I'm sorry, Ms Calwin, I've another funeral shortly. I'd suggest you sit in the garden, but the weather's foul."

"It's okay; I've taken enough of your time already. Thank you for the beautiful service, my mother would have appreciated it." Shoving the soggy tissue in her coat pocket, she stood up, turning one last time to the catafalque where the coffin had previously been. The noise of her heels reverberated around the stone room, echoing her loneliness.

She ambled to the bus stop to head back home; home where her mother would no longer be waiting for her.

The streets in Hackney were often jammed with people running errands, going to work, doing the school run, and generally ignoring one another. Red buses trundled down the road, whilst motorbikes and cyclists threaded their way through the swollen gorge of cars, slicing through the billowing clouds of pollution.

After a ragged journey, she alighted in front of the block of flats finding the rain had reduced to drizzle. Pulling her scarf tighter around her neck, she mooched towards the entrance.

Stepping inside the dingy foyer, she wandered over to the row of gunmetal mailboxes, to find a letter from the opticians reminding her mother to make an appointment. A tear budded in her eye, which she blinked back rapidly.

The lift was broken, forcing her to mount the three flights of concrete stairs to reach her flat. Once inside, the smell of lavender lingered in the air; a throwback of her mother's favourite perfume. As if spellbound by the scent, she moved towards her mother's bedroom and pushed the door wide open.

A handmade embroidered *J* hung over the bed. Alice had made it for her mother, Joy, for Mother's Day when she was ten years old. The walls were covered in faded floral wallpaper, and the view through the window was of an old church and adjoining cemetery. Joy would often say she was looking at her future neighbours, and vehemently believed her husband, Stan, would be waiting for her.

Alice opened the window to help rid the room of the lingering whispers of death. It had tickled her nose for days and now the final goodbye had been said, it was time for her to clean and de-clutter the flat and her mind.

In her own bedroom, a single bed stood against one wall, with a dressing table in front of the window. The view, in contrast to Joy's, overlooked the streets below. Regimented rows of dirty-brick Victorian houses built for the workers, with rabbit-hutch-size backyards running adjacent to the terraces. Some yards housed wheelie bins and broken plastic garden furniture, and others displayed old pots and containers, full of plants struggling to cope with the lack of sunlight and care. Empty washing lines rode the breeze like hammocks under palm trees.

The January sky over London was smudged with mucky clouds against a grey palette, matching her disposition perfectly as she reflected on her mother's last nine months; it was a relief when peace finally embraced her, as watching her suffer was soul destroying.

Alice's favourite room was the kitchen-diner, as the large window allowed natural light to flood in. She would sit for hours at the Formica table with her laptop, notebook, and large mug of coffee. The hours were only punctuated by the frequent demands of Joy, which Alice carried out with utmost care and diligence, as she felt a daughter should—especially one who had no life of her own to speak of. They had always been there for one another and their bond strengthened after her father died twenty years previously.

The kitchen walls were painted pale lemon, and the floor was covered in a black-and-white-check vinyl, which was cracked in various places after almost twenty years of wear. The cupboards were woefully outdated, and covered in a fine layer of grime that was so ingrained, no amount of sugar water would cleanse them.

The lounge had been rarely used since Joy became bed-bound four years previously. There was a sagging sofa with limp cushions strewn on it, and an upright armchair they had bought for Joy prior to her health deteriorating. A television sat unused under a layer of dust in one corner, and two walls were taken up with bookshelves, crammed with dog-eared paperbacks, mainly acquired from the sale shelves at the local library, and charity shops.

The thud of a bass beat shuddered through the wall; the neighbour's son was home from school. *And so it begins*, she thought, switching on the kettle and closing the kitchen door. Cocooned in that small space saved her sanity, but she was beginning to feel she was unravelling.

Sitting down with a mug of coffee, she flipped open the writers' magazine to be bombarded by numerous articles of authors' successes, and their advice on how to achieve the same. Their smiling faces beamed up at her, displaying the delight she had yet to experience, wondering if she ever would. Negative voices filled her head, gnawing at the fabric of her mind, distant memories begging to come out of the crevices to seep into her soul and blacken it forever.

Flicking to the back pages, she came across a plethora of adverts offering courses, editing services, and self-publishing packages. An advert for a writers' retreat in France caught her eye.

The coloured photograph depicted a timeworn chateaux surrounded by lavender bushes and olive trees. The mantle of cloudless sky was the blue of a new-born baby's eyes, and vines lay in regimented rows in the adjacent fields. It looked an idyllic place to escape to.

Her daydreaming was interrupted by the sound of a car horn. The closeness of the London hubbub crawled on her skin, mixing with the dust of the dead she sensed since leaving the crematorium. Leaving the magazine open, she left to have a shower.

Chapter 2

Ending the article with his name, Theodore Edwards, he e-mailed it to his boss before making a cup of Earl Grey tea.

The chill in the air was tempered by the open fire crackling and spitting in the grate. Theodore sat on the supple leather sofa and gazed at his garden which was shrouded in drizzle and overgrown with weeds intermingled with the established, albeit some dead, shrubs. He had fired the last gardener due to a personality clash, but he knew he needed to hire another one in the spring as he did not have the time, nor inclination, to do it himself.

Post thudded onto the door mat. Retrieving it, he discovered a letter from his estranged wife's solicitor, coating his face in a layer of sweat—a reaction any form of contact from Joanna, the mother of his only child, made. And that only child was finishing university in the summer. *Oh how time flies*, he mused.

He returned to the sofa and closed his eyes. He could feel another one of his headaches coming on. "A man my age shouldn't be under so much stress," he muttered under his breath.

He longed for a break, away from his vindictive soon-to-be ex-wife and away from London, which he was finding increasingly overwhelming and suffocating. He had rid himself of his car as parking spaces in Bethnal Green had become as rare as fairy dust, so he travelled everywhere by tube. The underground was not sanitized and air conditioned like the ones he travelled in New York, but rather cramped, stiflingly hot tin cans rattling along under the dusty streets of London.

A stack of novels leered at him from the coffee table; they required reviewing for *The Observer* newspaper. Normally he would be excited about being transported to the fictional worlds dreamt up by authors.

But today was different. He defied any novel to offer him the escapism he desired. Those days were gone.

Picking up a book magazine he periodically wrote for, a leaflet dropped out and rode gently on the movement of the air, landing gracefully at his feet. The photograph caught his eye.

Inspiration burgeoned in his mind, and suddenly all the gripes of his current life would be expunged; for a short while, at least.

"So Theo, what's this idea you've been so desperate to tell me about?" asked Charles Grover, the editor of the arts review section in the paper.

"Reviewing books has become a tad boring. I want to look at novels and writers from a new angle."

"And what angle would that be?"

"I attend a writers' retreat and do an article on the experience. I would go undercover, befriending the attending authors to get an insider's view of their aspirations and frustrations. What do you think?"

"And how much is this going to cost?"

"Only a matter a few hundred, on top of my fee, naturally."

"Naturally," mimicked Charles.

Theo pulled the leaflet from his messenger bag and pushed it across Charles's walnut veneer desk.

"France? I thought you'd have chosen a more exotic location."

"I want to go where ordinary people can afford to go, that way I should have more fascinating characters to write about. You know, the mum with too much time on her hands because the children are no longer at home, and her husband plays golf incessantly. Or an ordinary guy whose convinced he's the next Oscar Wilde."

Charles turned the leaflet over. "I'd want more than just one article. You could write a daily column so the readers can get acquainted with the writers over the week. What do you think?"

"Sounds great. Get your secretary to book it; the next one's in May." He disappeared from the office, leaving behind the musky scent of his cologne.

Theo managed to find a seat on the tube, surrounded by people trussed up in woolly hats and scarves. Padded jackets and duffle coats squished together, and his feet were becoming uncomfortably hot thanks to the vent belching-out heat from under his seat.

At the next stop, a large man threw himself into the vacant seat next to him. The man's elbow dug into his ribs, and their thighs resided side by side like caged chickens.

A rancid odour weaved its way to Theo's nostrils, emanating from his neighbour's damp wool coat which clearly hadn't been dry cleaned since the day it was bought. As the man fidgeted for space, his dampness rubbed against Theo's pristine English tweed coat. He made a mental note to take it to the drycleaners.

Once above ground again, he walked with his head bent down, the wind and rain buffering against the top of his head. Once upon a time his thick black hair would have protected his scalp. Now his thinning hair with flecks of grey offered more of a stubborn presence than protection.

Pounding the pavement, he bumped into someone outside his house. He muttered gruffly as he side-stepped them.

"As curmudgeonly as ever, I see."

Theo looked up, his eyes narrowing. "To what do I owe this unscheduled visit? Are you hand delivering your solicitor's letters now?"

"I'd rather step inside out of this god-awful rain."

Shrugging, he opened the front gate and fumbled for his door key before letting her in. He cared not that the hall was cluttered with various boots and coats. He liked to dress appropriately for each season, and leave the garments out as proof of his perfunctory nature.

"This mess is a sad commentary on the state of a single man," she said, scanning around.

"I don't suppose you'd care to tidy up whilst you're here," he replied with a lopsided grin.

"For goodness sake, Theodore. I want to get this divorce over and done with, but my solicitor says that you're not dealing with the paper-work at your end."

She strutted to the lounge and perched on the edge of the sofa, next to a pile of newspapers. He followed slowly behind, and leant his shoul-der against the door frame.

"I'm a rather busy man. I've handed over the nigh-on million-pound house, and you now have your own wealth, so why the desperation to have the divorce finalised?"

"Because I wish to re-marry and you're in my way."

His eyes widened at the news. He wondered what poor devil had the misfortune of linking his life with hers so soon.

She riffled around in her Mulberry handbag and retrieved a brown manila envelope, thrusting it in his direction. "Sign this and I'm out of your life."

"Except for when we attend Justin's graduation, and undoubtedly his future wedding." He wanted to ask how his son was, but did not want to hand her a metaphorical stick to thrash him with.

"We won't have to talk to one another at any of those events. An acknowledging nod will suffice."

He moved into the room and slid the paperwork from the envelope, placing the papers on the coffee table. He could smell Joanna's perfume in the room; she had always worn Chanel No19. He never liked it.

He retrieved his fountain pen from his messenger bag and scrawled his name on the document. "You're a free woman."

"What a relief, I'm finally going to be divorced from you."

"You really have no fond memories of our years together?"

Joanna searched the ceiling for an answer before she finally replied. "On reflection, no. You were an egocentric, stuffy man who was bla-tantly snobbish when it came to literature. I couldn't read a Jilly Cooper in front of you as you'd give me that meaning behind literature solilo-quy. You said I dumbed down our relationship with my small talk and lack of interests outside of childcare and shopping. Even when I started my own business, you belittled me and remained totally unsupportive, even when it took off. So no, I have no fond memories, apart from having Justin."

He heard her words but not what she was saying; dumbly watching her lips move just like he did throughout their marriage.

Standing up, she blew a kiss in his direction before almost skipping out of the house and out of his life.

Chapter 3

Alice felt bereft without her mother around. She cleaned the flat thoroughly and took her mother's clothes to the charity shop. She attended the hairdresser for a trim, but felt no relief from the emptiness, even on the two days she worked at a bakery. But a sense of guilt buffered her when she felt happy at having uninterrupted writing time.

With a mug of coffee and the weak spring sun shining through the kitchen window, Alice sat at the table with her laptop open, living a romantic life vicariously through her yet un-finished novel. Within the story she felt wanted, cherished, and loved. Reality had never bothered to open those doors for her again after her one and only sorry experience, leaving her jaded and scarred. Heat-seared welts slashed across her heart.

All this procrastinating was not getting her novel written, but she struggled to settle. She found herself subconsciously listening attentively in case her mother called for assistance. Whilst at other times, she frittered away hours scouring the bric-a-brac markets for kitsch items for the flat, or trawling charity shops and the library for yet more novels to devour.

She picked up the latest writing magazine from the table, and found the same advert for the writers' retreat in France. Before her nerves overpowered her, she picked up the phone and dialled the number.

"I believe the one in May is fully booked, madam. Oh no, wait . . . there's been a cancellation, you're in luck. France is so beautiful in May," said the woman.

After giving over her payment details, she flung herself on the sofa which groaned under her weight. She inhaled deeply a couple of times, before clapping her hands rapidly like an excited child staring into a toy shop window.

Grabbing a notepad and pen, she jotted down all the things she would need to take with her, as a smile surged across her face. "I've done it," she said aloud, "I've actually done it." She saw an image of her mother floating before her eyes, smiling proudly at her.

Theo picked up seven white linen shirts and seven pastel polo shirts from the racks before perusing a row of cravats. He decided the newspaper could afford to buy him a couple of new ones. Satisfied with his purchases, he strode off to his favourite wine bar in Covent Garden for a leisurely glass of Beaujolais whilst he continued reading a turgid novel on the life of a man who decided to live under the sea.

After his second large glass, he found his eyelids slowly closing and his chin dropping to his chest. He juddered awake at the sound of someone laughing at a nearby table. The book failed to enthral him so he rammed it back into his messenger bag and downed the last mouthful of wine.

A group of young women brushed past him, throwing their heads back and giggling. A redhead caught his eye, so he let a smile creep across his lips, but instead of smiling back, she scowled, flicking her hair over her shoulder and turning her back to him. He smiled wryly to himself, wondering whether he was beginning to look like a fool, an old fool at that. *Am I losing my touch?*

He'd always been aware of women around him, and it was his wandering eye and hands that caused the irreparable rift in his marriage. The rift swiftly became a cavern, and now he had an ex-wife with the bitterness of a vat of rotting lemons.

Joanna was an iconic beauty when they met at university. She had a slender figure, transparent blue eyes, and hair the colour of corn fields bathed in sunlight. They were the quintessential golden couple, envied by many and adored by all. Throughout their years at university they remained monogamous. It was easy for him back then, as she had a healthy appetite for sex and kept herself impeccably groomed.

The trouble started when the relationship merged into a matrimonial union, before progressing onto the damning phase of parenthood.

Joanna threw herself into being an earth mother. She developed an organic mother-and-baby range of beauty products, which she began selling to friends before branching out and selling in exclusive boutiques. Theo soon found himself relegated to the basement level in the pecking order. At just a few weeks old, Justin had overtaken Theo's role of man of the house. The little mite was an incontinent being who had no communication, apart from crying, and yet he held more command over Joanna than Theo ever had.

He contemplated buying another glass of red until a group of suited young men strutted the bar. He saw himself as being of a similar age, give or take a couple of years, but his delusion crumbled when he caught his reflection in the Rococo mirror on the crimson wall.

He promptly left, squeezing through the crowd with his shopping bags towards the tube to take him home.

He arrived at his front door to find his neighbour, Joyce, watering the winter pansies in her hanging basket.

"Goodness, you've been on a shopping spree," she called out.

"I'm off to France tomorrow. I've been meaning to ask you, could you feed Rufus for me whilst I'm away? I'll drop a spare key round in a bit."

"I'd be delighted to help. Holiday, is it?"

"No, it's an assignment for work."

"Oh, how exciting. I do love reading your reviews, and I always read the books you recommend and avoid the ones you don't." Joyce blushed furiously as she watched him disappear inside.

An open suitcase lay on his bed, ready to gobble up his new acquisitions. He packed his laptop in a separate work bag, and shoved in three novels he hoped to get through to review. Tomorrow could not come soon enough for him.

Chapter 4

Alice sat in the departure lounge, clutching her mustard-yellow leather handbag close to her chest, surrounded by couples and families with little children charging around. The sight pinched her heart for a few seconds.

Through the vast tinted windows, the sky appeared to be a murky mélange of blue and smoky-grey. She hoped the blue skies and sunshine in France would inspire her flagging word flow, and lift her out of the dank grave life had dug for her of late.

She noticed people sitting by themselves, just like her, and wondered if they were also heading to the retreat. Her heart began palpitating and an adrenaline rush was pushing her to run back to the safety of her flat. She closed her eyes and tried picturing herself somewhere peaceful and relaxing, hoping to regulate her breathing, when the announcement came for her to board the plane. *No turning back now.*

An orderly queue formed towards the desk where two polished-looking air hostesses stood, dressed in red fitted jackets and matching pencil skirts. Their lips shone with a glossy shade of crimson, and their hair was coiffed into a ballerina bun. Alice avoided eye contact as they wished her a happy flight.

The queue shuffled slowly down the tunnel like a dinner queue in a primary school until they reached the door of the plane. Alice found her seat and put her jacket in the overhead locker. Gripping her handbag, she slid past the first two empty seats and took her place next to the window, before shoving her bag under the chair. Shortly, the seats next to her were filled, and it wasn't long before the woman next to her began a conversation.

"I can't believe I'm finally getting away. I'm so excited."

Alice turned her head to face the woman and smiled, before returning her gaze to the window.

"Is this your first time flying?" persisted the woman.

"This isn't my first time, but I haven't flown for a long while."

"Are you nervous?"

"No, I'm fine, really." Alice spoke so quietly the woman had to lean in to hear her. Alice instinctively leant further towards the window.

Feeling rebuffed, the woman turned to the man on her left, who appeared more eager to converse. The couple soon got chatting about their grandchildren, and competing about who had the cleverest and most successful children. Alice was relieved to be left alone.

As the engines roared, she braced herself and watched the scenery speed passed the window, blurring the grey of the tarmac with the grey of the sky. The only colour to separate them was a strip of green, caused by the rows of conifer trees behind the tall wire fences. As they tipped back further and further, Alice gripped the armrests tightly, turning her knuckles white, resisting the urge to grab the woman's hand and tell her that she was indeed scared.

Theo thumbed through the pages of a novel until an air hostess with a trolley was within reach.

"Could I have a whiskey on the rocks?"

The hostess smiled, retrieving a small bottle before dropping two ice cubes in the plastic glass and handing it over, in exchange for cash.

The first sip warmed his throat, and aided the celebration of his getaway from the dismal shores of England. Then, the journalist within him kicked in, as he panned around eagerly to see if he could spot the aspiring authors amongst the passengers.

He was seated between a young woman who looked like a student and a man in his forties who was still wearing his seatbelt and whose hands were tightly pushed together in a prayer-like position. He had the window blind down.

"Are you heading to France for a vacation?" he asked the young woman.

"I'm visiting my boyfriend," she said, pulling her iPod from her rucksack and sticking the headphones in her ears.

Not for the writers' retreat, he noted mentally. He prayed Mister Nervous by the window was not either, and was majorly disappointed when Mister Nervous introduced himself as Clive Morris, an aspiring author, "In the flesh."

"I'd love to talk about my novel; it would take my mind off flying," he said excitedly.

"So you're heading for the writers' retreat?"

"Why yes I am. You too?"

"You've guessed it. Perhaps we should discuss your book at the retreat though, so I can experience the reveal along with everybody else."

Clive's initial look of disappointment transformed into a conspiratorial regard between them, as he tapped the side of his nose twice and winked before returning his hands to the prayer position. *Please let there be some young women there*, Theo said in his own offering to the gods. He decided to close his eyes lest Mister Nervous decide to impart his, no doubt scant, knowledge of the cut and thrust of querying agents and the dreaded synopsis.

Annoyingly, images of his ex-wife floated across his eyes, looking like she did when they first met. He pried his eyes open and requested another drink.

After everyone had collected their luggage from the churning carousel, they walked into the arrival's lounge to find a man standing by the railings with a sign saying "Lavender Writers' Retreat." A small group of people broke away from the mass of passengers, and finally Theo got the first glimpse of his fellow companions for the week. He spied only one young woman, but there was also a man similar in age to her. Theo doubted his chances in the competition that was bound to ensue. His overall impression was of overwhelming disappointment.

He counted three men and four women of indeterminate ages. He thought he was about to embark on the longest week of his life, and was relieved he'd purchased a large bottle of whiskey in the duty-free shop.

The group followed their guide in a crumpled beige suit, who was holding the sign aloft. The two older women, who had travelled together, were chattering excitedly, whereas the rest of the group shuffled along in silence, breathing in the start of their adventure as though every sight and smell would re-kindle their creative juices and bathe their souls in inspiration.

Chapter 5

No one sat together on the minibus except for the two travelling companions, Enid and Doris. As if to preserve their anonymity, everyone else gazed out the windows, watching the alien landscape forged against a canopy of turquoise, as it flashed passed them.

Bordeaux had once been considered a sleepy wine-producing area, with little to offer the discerning traveller, except those with a penchant for vintage wine. But over the past two decades, it had cleaned up its immense swaths of eighteenth-century architecture, and sculpted the riverbanks bordering the Garonne. In the centre of the town, an elegant opera house stood on the Place de la Comédie.

The two women spotted an artisan market in the square, and their excited noises made everyone follow their gaze. The men rolled their eyes, as the women voiced their desire to buy a few souvenirs over the coming week.

It was a short journey to the retreat which sat on the edge of the town of Bordeaux. The chateaux nestled between a vast expanse of vineyards, with their regimented rows stretching to the horizon on one side, and another field of regimented olive trees. As the minibus drove up the dusty track to the chateaux, the origin of the retreat's name became apparent, as mounds of billowing lavender bushes filled the front garden. The building had a decaying façade, looking like an ongoing project rather than the finished article.

"*Et voila*," announced the driver, pulling hard on the hand brake. "*Nous sommes ici*."

That was the first time he had spoken. Jumping out of the minibus, he slammed the door so everyone rocked in their seats, before sliding back the passenger door to let them dismount.

"I just know I'm going to love it here," declared Doris to anyone who cared to listen.

"Oh yes, dear, me too," gushed her white-haired friend.

How can they tell from here? Theo thought, standing up and promptly banging his head on the metal roof. Clive Morris jumped at the sound, and the young woman stifled a laugh.

The luggage was dumped unceremoniously on the dusty gravel by the front door as a woman bounded out of the chateaux, smiling and waving enthusiastically.

"*Bien venue*, welcome, one and all," she called out as they all shielded their eyes against the midday sun.

"I'm Maggie, and I'm your hostess for the week. You'll have to forgive Marcus for not being here, he's just gone to the wine merchant."

Maggie pointed to the elderly ladies. "Help the ladies, please, Pierre."

Clearly English was not a problem for him as he carried out her request, albeit begrudgingly. Enid and Doris followed behind with tiny steps, scuffing up the dust around their feet so they looked like they were walking on dirty clouds.

They all collected their bags and headed inside, where the temperature cooled markedly due to the thick stone walls and high ceilings, all painted white.

"If you'd all like to follow me I'll take you to your rooms." Her voice echoed around the space, along with exhausting enthusiasm.

They followed her up a flight of wide stone stairs. The sound of heels on the stone steps ricocheted around the walls, perhaps emphasizing why Maggie wore mink-coloured suede ballet pumps.

The first door they came to was the twin room for Enid and Doris. Pierre took their cases in, slinging them heavily at the end of each single bed. He gave a curt nod to the ladies before disappearing.

The room next door was given to the youngest woman in the group. Zoe stepped in and walked up to the window. "This view is awesome. Inspirational, in fact," she said, turning to smile at Maggie.

Alice had the next room. Draping across the glass double-doors, was a white muslin curtain, and beyond that was a small balcony encased by a wrought-iron railing, just large enough for a table and a chair.

Across the landing was the corridor where all the men were to reside. The first room was a single room for Clive. Walking in, he looked around rapidly, taking in his new surroundings before feeling the firmness of the mattress.

Next to him was another single room for Theo. And finally, the last room was a double room with a large four-poster bed, suitable for Marlon's build. He smiled at the opulent space as he placed his writing bag on the wooden desk.

"If you'd all like to freshen up and settle in, I'll go and prepare some lunch. Come down when you're ready and have drinks on the patio out the back." She bounded downstairs silently, leaving everyone in peace.

Alice rolled her shoulders and unpacked her clothes before placing her writing accoutrement on the white painted wooden desk which nestled in the corner of her room. Anxiety was clambering towards her mind at the thought of going downstairs to socialise with a group of strangers, fearing her inferiority in every aspect of life compared to them.

She scrutinised her reflection in the antique mirror on the wall, staring at the unfamiliar person peering back at her. Aspects of her mother had become more apparent; her tiny ears and pronounced Cupid's bow. However, the dullness in her eyes was reminiscent of her mother's last few weeks. Gripping her handbag, she descended the stone stairs.

She was not the first to arrive on the patio. Standing by the trestle table, was the tall black man, with muddy-brown soulful eyes, and eyelashes women crave to have. When he saw her looking at him, he smiled a smile that echoed a thousand greetings.

"Hi," he said with his arm extended, "I'm Marlon."

Alice took his hand which dwarfed hers. "Alice."

There was an awkward pause between them, and Alice prayed she could think of something to say, but only an empty hum resonated around her mind.

"What genre do you write?" he finally asked.

"Romance; and you?"

"Sci-fi." He saw her blank expression. "Science-fiction."

Alice nodded, giving the briefest smile, before they heard footsteps approaching.

"So this is where everyone is. I'm Zoe," said the vibrantly-dressed young woman.

After the introductions, Marlon picked up the carafe and poured three glasses of red.

"*Santé,*" he said as he raised his glass.

"You speak French?" quizzed Zoe.

"Just the odd word here and there."

"I love your accent. Where are you from?" Zoe was a bubbling fountain of questions.

"South Africa. I came to Britain to study and decided to stay."

"Awesome."

All the while the pair were talking, Alice slowly backed away into the shadows by the wall. The coolness of the stone was soothing against her back, feeling like a caress. It had been years since she felt anything akin to that.

Voices came from the room behind her, before Maggie came into view with the rest of the group.

"Do help yourself to wine. We also have fruit juice if anyone would prefer." Maggie ushered people towards the glasses before disappearing to the kitchen to finish lunch.

"We meet again, neighbour," Clive said to Theo.

At first Theo's mind was blank, and then he remembered. "Mister Nervous," he muttered under his breath.

"Pardon?"

"Nothing," he replied quickly.

"We're outnumbered by the women, aren't we?" Clive continued, wringing his hands in front of his paunch.

"Maybe in number, but not in aptitude, I shouldn't wonder."

Enid and Doris scuttled over, and the conversation was as dull as Theo expected. He berated himself for not drinking a couple of whiskeys in his room before joining the group.

He watched Marlon talking to Zoe with a soupcon of envy. Earlier he had overheard Marlon bragging about being the only guy in the group with a chance with her.

It was then that the mouse-like woman standing in the shade caught his eye. He did not remember seeing her on the plane, or on the minibus come to that. Although she was not his type, he thought she might be a distraction, so he strode up to her and introduced himself.

"Alice," she replied quietly.

"Are you writing a novel or short stories?"

"A novel, a romantic novel."

Theo wanted to voice *quelle surprise* but thought better of it.

"And what genre novel are you writing?" she asked, pleased with herself.

"I'm not writing one. I'm a short-story man, myself."

"And you've come on a retreat to write a short story?" Alice blushed, looking at his shoes rather than his face.

"I didn't think the retreat had an admission criteria."

"Gracious no, sorry, I didn't mean to imply anything by that."

Theo watched her wilt under the pressure of socializing. Her *faux pas* had slapped her in the face, and he felt he should rescue her, but to what end?

"What are you hoping to gain from this week?" He tried to soften his voice, but instead it came out rather like a pimp cajoling a new recruit.

"Help yourselves to lunch," Maggie called out, indicating the feast laid out on the trestle table. No one had noticed her ferrying baskets of baguette, bowls of black olives and endives, platters of cold meats and smoked salmon, pâté, brie, fruit, and a bowl of cold runner beans drizzled with crushed garlic and olive oil.

Both Theo and Alice felt secretly relieved at being rescued by Maggie. He separated himself from her in three strides of his sinewy elongated legs, finding himself in close proximity to the vivacious Zoe.

She smelt of vanilla and burnt sugar, an intoxicating mix for any man's nose. His nostrils flared filling his lungs. He was so lost in the moment he did not feel her nudging him with the edge of a plate.

"I'm Zoe. Do you want a plate, man with no name?"

Theo exhaled, taking the plate whilst introducing himself. They strolled alongside the table, loading their plates with the culinary delights of French cuisine.

"Is this your first time at a writers' retreat?" he ventured.

"Yes, and I'm really excited. I wanted to get away from the noise of life, to submerge myself in the written word." She popped an olive into her mouth letting her fingers linger at her lips. "If it was noise of the carnal type it would help me with my writing. I write erotica short stories and I've started a novel in the same genre." She gazed up at him with her pea-green eyes.

"Interesting."

"Sorry, old man, could you pass me the plate of cured meats?" Marlon said, towering over Theo, which was not a frequent occurrence in his everyday life.

He was irked by the interruption, the malice behind the adverb, and the fact that Marlon had overlooked the very British etiquette of queuing. Begrudgingly he handed his adversary the plate, trying not to ram it into his taut torso. "I'll give you 'old man,'" he muttered under his breath as he bobbed up and down on the balls of his feet, like a pigeon on heat.

Tables were dotted around the patio, some in the sun and others in the shade. Once her plate was full, Zoe headed for the sun and Marlon was quick to follow. Only Theo hesitated where to sit.

He weighed up his options. He could sit with the old dears, but then he would look like he had taken a seat in God's waiting room. He was too angry to sit with Marlon and Zoe, even though he was already getting withdrawal symptoms of her scent. Timid Alice was seated near an olive tree on her own, and Clive was anxiously looking where to eat until he caught Theo's eye. The corner of Clive's mouth twitched as he mouthed some form of invitation to him. In desperation, Theo darted towards Alice's table, startling her as he let his plate thud on the table.

"May I join you both?" panted Clive, arriving swiftly after Theo.

Neither rushed to accept, but without waiting for their consent, he dropped into a chair.

"I think we've split into our cliques already, by the looks of things," he said in a hoarse whisper. "The old ladies who came together and the young have teamed-off together. He's a handsome devil, if I say so myself."

"And how do you see us?" questioned Theo.

"We're the middles; neither old nor yet that young, if you pardon my bluntness," he said towards Alice. "I mean, I'm forty-seven, you look about fifty-five, and I wouldn't dare guess a ladies age."

"Actually I'm not for the scrap heap just yet, I'm only fifty-two," muttered Theo.

"And I'm only in my early forties," piped up Alice before taking bird sips of wine.

"As I said, we're in between the others," Clive repeated before biting into a chunk of baguette loaded with brie and grapes.

He made chomping noises, which Alice found off-putting, and she wondered if Theo did too, as she peered at him from under the protection of her fringe.

Clive was a juxtaposition of anxiety and rudeness, with neither trait dominating his character. Alice found the mixture unappealing, and she was sorry he was sitting there at all. Theo, on the other hand, intrigued her, albeit he was eight years older than her. But what did age matter once you hit forty?

He was a difficult man to work out. He was clearly stylish with his white linen shirt and pale blue trousers, making his appearance more casual rather than contrived. She noticed his penchant for the younger woman of the group, and how he appeared bored in her company. His brusque manner could be construed as uncharitable and callous.

Clive, on the contrary, dressed ostentatiously in white billowing trousers and a pistachio-coloured silk shirt, matching his flamboyant mannerisms. He frequently dabbed his perspiring face with a mono-grammed handkerchief, which he retrieved from his top pocket with a flourish.

"I found out that the two elderly women, Enid and Doris, write his-torical romance and detective fiction. However, guess what the delecta-ble Marlon writes?" he asked, his eyes dripping with conspiratorial glee.

Alice knew but did not care to say.

"He writes science-fiction, which isn't a genre I usually read, but I might just make an exception where he's concerned. He does have magnificent biceps." Clive shovelled a forkful of salad into his rubbery mouth.

"I think Zoe may have dibs on Marlon's biceps," Theo said, with a sly grin. He was going to enjoy winding up Mister Nervous.

They concluded the meal with fresh nectarines and figs, whilst Mag-gie brought out a couple of pots of coffee, along with delicate bone china cups and saucers. The men were unable to fit their finger and thumb through the handle, so they cradled the cups instead.

"Ah, my husband finally makes an appearance. This is Marcus," announced Maggie.

Marcus sported a floppy fringe and high cheekbones. His teeth glowed brightly as he smiled at the entourage.

"I trust you're all settled in, and hopefully we'll provide you with the peace and sustenance you all need to keep your words flowing." He spoke clearly and enunciated well, as though speaking to a group of foreigners.

The group rumbled with positive affirmations, satisfying him enough to peck Maggie on the cheek before heading back inside.

One by one, they began standing up and stretching their legs. Mag-gie invited people to sit anywhere in the grounds or inside the chateaux.

Writing tables and chairs were even located in the sparsely stocked library, and in the airy sitting room. Everyone had a desk in their bedroom, and those people lucky enough to have a balcony could move theirs out there. People were free to move tables around if they preferred to sit with other writers rather than be in solitude.

Marcus and Maggie Bolt-Smith had tried to think of everything where their retreat was concerned; they needed the business to work. Marcus used to be a city trader in Canary Wharf, and with his bonus bought the chateaux to run when he took early retirement. After the banking crisis, he took the early retirement and they packed up their London life and moved to France, only to find the chateaux required more extensive renovation once they began peeling off the wallpaper.

Feeling the pressure, they decided to have paying guests to stay at the same time as renovating. Naturally, for the purposes of the retreat, the only work taking place was that of re-plastering and painting the fractured walls, and Marcus was doing the work himself.

Alice scuttled up to her room, having had enough company for a while. Besides, she was keen to use her own balcony, hoping the view would awaken her dormant writing muse.

The heat outside had become intense, and it was a relief when she opened her bedroom door to be greeted by a more ambient temperature, and to find her balcony was in the shade.

Theo bolted for his room to get away from Clive. On reflection, he thought Clive may be just the person to lure Marlon away from Zoe long enough for him to make his move. He had a feeling she might be tempted by the more mature, and obviously richer, man.

Opening his laptop, he made notes on the numerous characters and their quirks, his fingers flitting over the keyboard like a kingfisher swooping across a river, witty comments racing through his brain making him chuckle. The title of his first column was simply, "Arrival Day."

Whilst working, the sound of laughter drifted into his room through the window; it sounded like Zoe's throaty laugh. Intrigued, he moved to the open window and peered through the cream lace curtains, but he could not see her. Then she laughed again. This time, he stuck his head around the window to see her sitting on Marlon's balcony. So not only had the swine got the only double bed, he had a balcony too. That was too much for Theo.

Delving into his suitcase, he fished out the bottle of whiskey before pouring it into a glass he found by the sink. He would forgo the ice cubes, such was his desperation.

"You do make me laugh, Marlon," Zoe said, flicking her raven hair over her shoulder. "Maybe humour should be your genre?"

"Perhaps I'll consider it after this book's finished." He stretched across the table to grasp her hand.

She moved it away and smiled. "There's no rush is there?"

He sat back in his seat and rubbed his shoulder. "I think it's a bit stiff, probably missing my gym sessions," he said, disregarding her rebuff.

"Is that why your body is in such good shape?" She cast her eyes over him quickly. "Maybe I can help you with an exercise regime during the week?"

He winked in response.

"I must go, you've given me plenty of ideas to write about," she smiled.

"Hopefully we can put those ideas into practice very soon."

Chapter 6

After a day of intensive writing, deleting, and rewriting, everyone gathered in the evening for aperitifs on the patio. Canapés of fish eggs and cream cheese were placed on pure white china plates to tempt the guests whilst they drank sparkling white wine.

Zoe wore a dark purple satin cat suit, with open-toed wedge sandals. Her black hair was tied up in a loose bun, with tendrils caressing the nape of her neck. Marlon, who could not take his eyes off her, wore tight black jeans and a black muscle top which emphasized every curve and sweep of his chest. Even the two elderly women were appreciating the view.

"I say, he's a bit of eye candy," cooed Clive, quietly sidling up to Theo. "He could be my muse. I must get a photo of him before the week is over." He grinned at Theo who remained stoically mute.

Out of the corner of his eye, Theo spotted Alice hovering by the patio doors, gazing upon the scene as if she were a stagehand. He thought about rescuing her from her position when Maggie arrived with a flourish and invited the guests to take their seats in the dining room.

They may have been the elders of the group, but where food was concerned, Enid and Doris moved like le Mistral. Everyone else sauntered inside like ducklings following their mother. Marlon was a permanent fixture next to Zoe, and Clive had bagged the role of limpet to Theo. Only Alice took silent, solitary steps as she moved towards a table in the corner.

"Mind if we join you," chirped Clive as he stood over Alice.

She looked up and saw Theo towering above Clive, rolling his eyes.

"Of course; although I can't guarantee scintillating conversation."

Clive was oblivious to her response, preferring to choose a seat where he could see Marlon on the other table. Theo watched the pantomime before taking the free seat.

Maggie brought out the starter of homemade tomato soup with rustic French bread, and Marcus arrived with carafes of local red wine, placing one on each table. He was not as keen as his wife about social chit-chat, so he just nodded as he visited each table. Alice felt a pang for his obvious discomfort.

Maggie returned a while later to scoop the crockery away. Although she was smiling, her face glowed like a vine tomato covered in morning dew. The aroma of rosemary and garlic drifted in from the kitchen, as conversation flowed in the room.

"So Alice," began Clive, "tell us a bit about yourself."

Alice crushed her hands together in her lap, sensing a dappling rash mounting from her chest. She sensed the men's eyes scouring her face for secrets. *What am I to say?*

"I've nothing exciting to mention, my life's quite dull. I imagine your lives are far more entertaining."

"No romantic liaison to impart?" Clive urged.

Alice shook her head. How could she say she also had no career to speak of; that she lived her life vicariously through her writing? Would they understand?

Clive was impatient. "Well I've just met this delectable ballet dancer. He came to my chiropody clinic and it was love at first foot scrub. His body is to die for," he sighed, before picking up his wine glass. "What about you, Theo?"

"I'm recently divorced. It would appear you're the only one who ticks the relationship box."

Clive sat back like a petulant child. "It would seem that I've picked the wrong table to sit at. I may have to bail out and hitch a ride with the mighty Marlon and Zoe." He took a mauve handkerchief from his pocket and patted his brow and nose.

"I suspect you're not his type," said Theo, cocking his head in Marlon's direction.

"A man can dream," replied Clive with a subtle wink. "If he were gay, you could get your mitts on Zoe."

"Why don't we test that scenario? It could work for both of us."

"You're a sly dog," laughed Clive, playfully slapping Theo on the arm.

At his loud outburst, everyone turned towards them. Zoe could not help giving Theo a coquettish flash of her eyes, which did not go unnoticed by anyone at his table.

"Perhaps you *do* have a chance with her," whispered Clive in Theo's ear, so closely he felt his warm breath tickle the down-like hairs on his lobe.

Maggie trooped in with plates of rosemary and garlic encrusted lamb, followed by dishes of Puy lentils and baby sweet corn.

As Alice moved her foot under the table, she accidentally came into contact with Theo's. She muttered an apology under her breath, but he did not appear to have noticed.

The evening meal was rounded off with a dense chocolate mousse with a frozen mint leaf on top, and coffee. Marlon and Zoe were the first to finish, and the first to leave the dining room. A few minutes later, they walked past the open patio doors, wandering around the garden, deep in conversation.

"Perhaps we should move outside," Clive said to Theo.

"Pointless. I'm going to retire to my room to write." He stood up and nodded to the pair before striding upstairs to his awaiting bottle of whiskey.

Alice felt like a ghost hovering around the group. As she stood, no one noticed her, so she, too, disappeared to her room.

"It's a beautiful evening, I'm glad we're outside," said Zoe, linking her arm through Marlon's, feeling his muscles twitch on contact.

"I want to finish my novel this week, but I fear you're going to be a major distraction," he mused.

"I also have writing to do. We'll work during the day and relax at night. How does that sound?"

"Perfect, doll face."

"Why do you call me that?"

"Your porcelain face, big green eyes, and black hair. You'd be the perfect model for a porcelain doll."

"I guess that's a compliment. What do you do apart from writing and picking up women?"

"I'm a personal trainer."

"Ah, that explains your physique. Do you think I need a personal trainer?"

"We'll see." He arched an eyebrow before letting a broad grin drag across his face.

Chapter 7

Theo poured a large measure of whiskey into the glass containing a couple of ice cubes he had pilfered from downstairs. The first mouthful rippled across his tongue as he opened his laptop and waited for it to boot up.

He had come up with a title to over-arch his columns, "A Week with the Wannabes." *Harsh but fair*, he thought, taking another swig before letting the words tumble from his mind.

My first meeting with the group didn't bring up any surprises. Firstly, the two elderly women who aspire to be the next Agatha Christie and Barbara Cartland, both seem to be cherishing the food and wine more than absorbing the literary atmosphere.

But who am I kidding. There is no literary atmosphere to speak of, nor whiff of underlying talent or future success. How do I know that, I hear you ask. I only have to listen to their inane babbling to see that eloquent words and evocative similes do not run through their brains.

A couple has already been formed, and I wonder how long it will be before I hear the vulgar sounds of copulation coming through the wall—I'm unfortunate enough to be in the adjacent room to the stallion.

And as for the last two misfits with whom I shared a table with tonight: The man is so focused on the muscles of the stallion, I can't imagine there's much space in his brain for composition, and I had to hold a laugh in when the timid woman who barely spoke said she was writing a romantic novel. Will she be describing heaving bosoms in the vein of Jane Austin, or will the protagonists never consummate their love, so that it remains pure, just like her own body probably is, I imagine.

I can't wait for the results of the writing sessions. I imagine people will be clamouring to boast of their word count and to read sections of their turgid work to the group.

All I can say is thank God I brought a large bottle of whiskey.

He pressed send, finished his drink, and closed the laptop. He was pleased with his first column and believed Charles would think the money was well spent when the week was over.

The peace was broken by the bubbly laughter of Zoe in the corridor. He waited for Marlon's bedroom door to open, but instead heard tapping at his door. He ran his hand over his hair as he walked to the door.

"I thought you'd still be up," she cooed.

He looked around her to see where Marlon was.

"He's been snared by that Clive guy. If you ask me, he's hot for Marlon. Good taste though." She paused to stifle a giggle. "Aren't you going to invite me in?"

Theo stood back and let her pass. She strolled around his room stroking the furniture and bed as she passed it. "You poor thing, you only have a single bed."

"One doesn't have need for a double here."

"Oh, does *one* only have a single at home too?"

"No I don't, and there's no need to mock me. You came to my room, remember?"

She blew him a kiss and mouthed an apology to him, before performing a pirouette then slamming her body against his chest, unbalancing them briefly.

"You're drunk. Perhaps you should have a coffee?"

"And here I was thinking you'd appreciate my company," she whimpered like a lapdog.

"I do, but I don't want to abuse the situation. I thought you were having a lovely evening with Marlon."

"I was. You know what? I'm going to drag Marlon away from that guy. At least he'll know how to treat a woman in his bedroom. Oh and he," she reached the door and opened it, "definitely has the need for a double bed." She closed the door firmly behind her before cantering down the corridor.

Enid and Doris sat under a pagoda in the dusky light. They were sure Marlon and Zoe would end up in a passionate clinch, so they were bitterly disappointed when Zoe moved inside, thanks to interfering Clive.

They watched the two men walk side by side. Clive brushed his hand along the lavender, then smelt his palm.

"What do you think they're talking about?" asked Doris.

"Goodness knows. They can't have much in common."

"Well I say it's a shame for the young folk . . . Oh wait, she's back." Enid tempered her excitement lest they should be discovered.

They watched Zoe zigzag across the patio before crunching over the gravel towards the men, who jumped apart as she reached them.

"You've ignored me long enough, Marlon. Let's go to your room," she said, standing on tiptoes and just managing to drape her hands around his neck to hang like a necklace.

"My, you smell like a pub floor," said Clive, wrinkling up his nose.

"And you look like an unwanted, decaying wedding cake."

They eyed one another ferociously, and somewhere in Zoe's throat a growl formed.

"Now, now children," Marlon said, placing a hand on each of their shoulders. "We're all tired, and a little tipsy. Let's all go to bed so we can tackle our writing tomorrow."

"I thought you'd never ask," she whispered.

"I meant to our own beds, doll face."

She stamped her foot so gravel dust puffed around her ankles. Marlon took her by the hand and guided her back inside.

"Let's go in, Doris, the show's over."

The pair eased themselves off the bench, shuffling inside as deep fatigue suddenly engulfed them.

Marlon took Zoe up to her room. She turned and leant against the door. "Your bed would be more comfortable."

"It's only the first night, doll face. Let's get a good night's sleep. I'll see you at breakfast." He put his arms to either side of her head, bent down, and kissed her on the lips. It was quick, but firm. "Treat them mean, keep them keen," he murmured before moving away.

Chapter 8

Alice awoke to warm tentacles of sun slipping through the slats in the shutters. Her limbs were entangled in the quilt as though it were another body, but made from more luxurious bedding than she was used to. Momentarily disorientated, she opened her eyes and drank in the beautiful room before anxiety bubbled to the surface as she remembered the rest of the group.

Gathering her wash bag and towel, she opened the door and peered down the corridor before creeping out and heading for the bathroom. The room was spacious with peeling white paint on the walls, and blue-and-white tiles running along the side of the basin and shower, which was large enough to fit two people underneath. Maggie had warned that the flagstone floor risked becoming slippery.

The water beat a gentle rhythm on her scalp. Closing her eyes, she let it trickle down her face like the tears of a lost soul she carried around with her. Visions of her mother permeated her thoughts, bringing with them the joys of early childhood and the heartache of recent years.

Joy had wanted her daughter to find love whilst she was still alive. She hoped to see her get married, but Alice's timidity and low self-esteem had prevented her from venturing down that road. Unbeknown to Joy, Alice had made tentative steps at one point, but she was so badly crushed by the experience, she felt she could never trust another man. Ever.

With a towel wrapped around her head and her flimsy dressing gown doing its best to cover her body, she opened the door to find Enid standing there.

"I didn't mean to startle you," apologized Enid, seeing her jump. "You missed a treat last night. Zoe got tipsy, seemingly annoyed that Marlon and Clive had become a bit chummy. I can't wait to see how they all behave today."

"Hopefully everyone will be writing," replied Alice, finding her voice.

"If you ask me, any woman writing erotica is bound to be consumed with the notion of sex." She arched an eyebrow and pursed her lips.

"We don't know that for sure," smiled Alice. "I'll see you at breakfast." Clutching her robe tightly around her, she dashed back to her room.

After dressing, she pushed back the wooden shutters to let the fresh air surge into the room, billowing the muslin nets. She dabbed a muted brown lipstick on her lips before making her way downstairs.

Clive was already seated outside, sipping his coffee. "Good morning. Sleep well?"

"I did. Are you ready to write today?" she asked, taking a seat at an adjacent table.

"My fingers are itching to get going."

"What did you say you were writing?"

"A thriller." He broke off a piece of warm croissant and smothered it with butter before popping it into his mouth. A worm-like sliver of grease crept from his bottom lip.

"Are you looking for a peer review or critique whilst you're here?" she asked.

"No, I prefer to work alone. Why, are you?"

"I think I'll take the opportunity if it comes up. I don't attend a writers' group back home, so it might be useful to get feedback here." She paused as Maggie placed a coffee and warm croissant in front of her. "Would you be interested in giving me feedback?" she asked, turning back to him.

"I know absolutely nothing about the romance genre. I don't think I'd be useful."

"Any writer can give constructive criticism on any genre. You'd be looking at sentence structure, pace, and so on."

He shrugged before putting another chunk of croissant in his mouth.

"The accounts aren't panning out," Marcus muttered as he sat at the kitchen table.

"Now is not the time, darling. Can we discuss this after I've done the breakfasts?" Maggie's flushed face was gleaming with a thin veil of sweat.

"There's always something for you to do in this damn place. We have to talk sooner or later."

"Keep your voice down. Could you put the kettle on to boil again please?"

"You work very hard for very little reward."

"Any new venture is hard work in the beginning. Once this place is completely refurbished and word of mouth gets out, we'll soon see what a pleasant lifestyle we've carved out for ourselves, especially when we employ staff."

Marcus gazed through the kitchen window, admiring the azure sky void of any clouds. When they arrived ten months ago, they were bursting with enthusiasm and energy. But the more they tried to renovate the chateaux, the more work they found needed doing.

Maggie never lost faith in their abilities or the appeal of the place, but Marcus was finding money worries eating away at his happiness; putting trepidation in its place and inertia replacing energy.

"Rather than standing there doing nothing, why don't you give me a hand and see if anyone else has arrived for breakfast?"

He disappeared then returned saying they were just waiting for two. Maggie sighed before straightening her apron. "Onwards and upwards," she muttered to herself.

Zoe sat with Alice for breakfast, much to her surprise.

"I've got a monster of a hangover. Where's the damn coffee," she said hoarsely.

"Marcus was here a minute ago. I'm sure he won't be long," replied Alice, trying to see where Zoe was looking from behind her sunglasses.

"I feel ghastly," she said, digging around in her handbag to retrieve a box of headache tablets. She sloshed water from the glass jug into a tumbler before popping two in her mouth.

When Maggie finally arrived with her coffee, Zoe requested two slices of toast.

"We only have baguette or croissant."

"I can only stomach toast and black coffee when I'm like this."

Maggie sighed surreptitiously, and Alice noticed a sadness in her eyes.

"Are you planning on writing today?" Alice ventured quietly.

"Once my head is sorted. I've re-read the manuscript and I don't think its erotic enough in places." She paused to sip the steaming black liquid. "I need a couple of un-interrupted hours to work in more sex scenes."

Maggie brought a couple of slices of hot buttered baguette, opened out flat, to the table, for which Zoe muttered her appreciation.

A heavy silence shrouded the pair. Alice picked up the croissant and opened it with her fingers before layering it with butter. She looked around the room, noticing how the rest of the group were interacting with one another.

"Are you hoping for a bit of romance whilst you're here?" asked Zoe suddenly, as she dusted crumbs from the corner of her mouth.

"No, I'm here to write. Why, are you?"

"I always try and pep things up if I go on a retreat or residential course. It gives me so much material for my writing." She nibbled on the baguette like a guinea pig nibbling on celery. "I can't believe my luck to have two male muses here."

"Room for one more?" asked Theo, standing above the table.

"This is what I'm talking about, do join us," she purred.

He pulled out a chair and sat down. Maggie was quick to his side with a coffee.

"Sleep well, ladies?"

"I was a little lonely, but apart from that it was okay," Zoe answered, peeking over the top of her sunglasses.

"Fine thanks," Alice whispered, even though she knew he had stopped listening.

Finally Marlon arrived to complete the group. He surveyed the tables and waited until Zoe had seen him before taking a seat at the other end of the room.

Maggie coughed. "At ten thirty, I'll provide coffee, fruit, and pastries in here. Help yourselves, and take it to where you're writing if you wish."

"When I can get going," Zoe said, playing with her glass of water.

"Lunch is at one, afternoon tea at five, and the evening meal at eight. If there is anything else we can do, just let us know."

A murmur of appreciation rumbled around the room as Maggie returned to the kitchen.

"Where are you going to write?" Zoe asked Alice.

"On the balcony in my room. The view is picturesque."

Zoe pulled a face as though sucking on lime. "What about you?" she said, turning to Theo.

"I'll find some space in the shade somewhere. Away from everyone."

"Well aren't you two dull. I need people round me for inspiration. Preferably good-looking men."

"Pity you've only got Marlon and me then."

"If you're fishing for compliments, it won't work—" She was interrupted by the sight of Marlon leaving the dining room. She pushed the remainder of bread to one side, and gulped down her coffee before swiftly following him.

"You don't have to stay, I'm fine alone," said Alice.

"I'd like to finish my breakfast if you don't mind."

"Oh no, I meant—"

"I know exactly what you meant. You worry too much."

She stared at him for as long as she dared, trying to figure out whether he was joking or cross, before staring into her coffee cup whilst he finished eating.

The sound of cups being returned to saucers and chairs scraping along the floor alerted Alice that it was time to leave. As she stood up, Theo wished her a successful writing session. "Same to you," she smiled.

Chapter 9

From her balcony, Alice watched Theo stride towards a table under a mimosa tree. He looked tiny from where she was sitting. He carried a battered leather messenger bag and wore a panama hat, giving him the ability to blend in and yet retain his individuality. She envied that.

A noise from the garden distracted her. Zoe was cooing and waving to Theo as she strolled arm in arm with Marlon.

"Everyone is being so . . . diligent about writing," Zoe said huskily.

"This *is* a writing retreat. We've all come here with goals and expectations. All except you, it would seem," Marlon replied.

"I have those too. I just need to be around people, especially people like you."

Marlon found a table in the shade and pulled it into the dappled sunshine, setting down his notebook and pen. Zoe pulled the chairs across and sat down.

"What's it with you and that older guy?" he asked.

"You mean Theo?" She twirled a strand of hair around her finger. "Why, are you jealous?"

"I've got nothing to be jealous about, doll face. I just can't work you out. Perhaps you're looking for a father figure or a sugar daddy?"

"I'm the quintessential enigma," she beamed. "Perhaps you should get to know me better?"

"I'd like to, but I'd also like to get some writing done. I'm busy at work and knackered by the time I get home. This is a golden opportunity for me to get plenty of chapters written."

"You're so boring," she replied, folding her arms across her stomach. "Anyway, what's with you and that Clive? I think he's got a crush on you, you'd better watch out."

Marlon pointed gruffly to his notebook, so she puckered her lips and blew him a kiss before walking back to the chateaux, swaying her body to and fro, in case Marlon—or even Theo—was watching her.

Watch This Space

I had fun watching the group take their first breakfast together. A young woman—let's call her Zara—arrived with an almighty hangover, and could barely manage her black coffee and toasted baguette. She spends most of her time flirting with either myself (who can blame her?) or a younger man more her age (but no more of a man than yours truly). She was disappointed when he didn't take her to bed last night, but if you ask me, their sweaty bodies will be writhing together before the end of the week.

The woman writing a romantic novel—let's call her Anna—is almost too afraid to speak, and looks like she would faint if a man were to enter her bedroom, let alone her body. I imagine her body knows nothing of the touch of a man, so the mind boggles at how that might translate in her novel.

The two elderly ladies—I'll call them Dana and Elsie—barely appear on my radar due to their extreme dullness. One man—whom I'll call Mark— preens himself to perfection and puffs out his chest as Zara walks by. Watching the pair as they circle each other waiting to see who'll make the first move is fascinating. Anna should take notes; she'd be writing a more believable novel than I wager she is right now.

The last man—whom I'll call Colin—is attracted to Mark, and he does his best to flock to him whenever he can. He and Zara are competing for the same man; what a joy to observe.

I want to get to know Anna more, as I sense she has a dark secret, hence the dearth of romance in her life. Watch this space.

As Theo sent his next column to Charles, he had the familiar feeling of smugness rushing over him that he used to experience when he first started working at the paper. He believed the series would rejuvenate his career and his spotlight in the paper. He had a good feeling about it.

Clive bit into a succulent peach, feeling the furry skin on his tongue as the juice overflowed his lips and dribbled down his chin. Pulling out a monogrammed handkerchief, he dabbed his mouth.

Marlon appeared on the patio with his coffee. He acknowledged Clive with a curt nod, to which Clive offered a wide smile and a flourishing wave of his handkerchief.

"We meet again," said Zoe, sidling up to Marlon with her coffee and a pastry. "Fancy the shade or the sun?"

"The heat's getting a bit intense, I'm sticking to the shade for now."

She pulled out a chair, and sat with him underneath the wooden veranda that had vines wrapped around the structure. The dappled sunlight bounced off her mirror-shine hair, as she watched him over the brim of her cup, drinking in his stature. She could almost taste the salty sweat coating his face like a fine layer of bubble-wrap.

"It's a little freaky when you just stare at me, doll face."

His words broke her daydream. She broke off a small piece off the pastry before slowly placing the morsel into her mouth.

"Have you actually done any writing this morning?" he asked.

"I have. In fact I'm so inspired by you, I've changed my male protagonist to a South African. It suits him better somehow."

"Glad I've been of service."

"Perhaps I've become your muse?"

"I don't believe in that theory. It's too easy to blame a muse for writer's block, rather than actually bearing the responsibility yourself."

Sucking in a deep breath and exhaling slowly, Zoe looked around. Everyone else was also ensconced in the shade, whilst Maggie scampered around like an agitated terrier to check all was okay. Theo was engaged in conversation with the two elderly women. It was then that she noticed Clive, peering at her over the book he was feigning to read.

"There's something odd about that Clive. He definitely comes across as gay, but he can't keep his eyes off me. What do you think that's all about?"

"How should I know?" he snapped. "You do ask some idiotic questions at times."

After cramming the last morsel of pastry in her mouth, she stood up then paused, but when he ignored her, she moved away, hoping he would call her back. He didn't.

"So ladies, what's the story behind you two?" Theo asked.

"Doris and I attended the same bridge club, then we started having coffee together once a week," replied Enid.

"We both wanted a new hobby," offered Doris, "so we chose writing."

"So this isn't a life-long dream to write a book then?"

The women chuckled. "At our time of life, we're happy to give anything a go, and who knows, we may have some talent." They tittered again.

"We're going to have a siesta. It's an age and heat thing, you know." Enid laughed as they semi-curtsied before scurrying inside.

Theo was disappointed, but not surprised about not gleaning more gossip. Looking around, he saw Alice sitting by herself reading a book, so he picked up his coffee cup and moved towards her.

"Mind if I sit with you?"

Alice looked up and smiled as she closed her book.

"I'm not disturbing you, am I?"

"I always find time for reading, but it's not a substitute for conversation."

"How's your writing coming along?"

"Stiltedly, I'm afraid. Perhaps I'm hoping for too much from this retreat." She fiddled with the handle of the coffee cup as her face grew scarlet.

"Perhaps we should sit together for dinner tonight so you can give me a synopsis of your book? I may be able to kick-start your word flow."

Alice dug her fingernails into the palm of her hand, willing her voice to remain steady.

"Well . . ."

"As promised, writers, I'm here to make sure you don't fritter away your hours socialising. Time to return to your manuscripts," Maggie called out.

Everyone stirred and moved inside where the air was cooler.

"See you at dinner," Theo smiled.

Alice nodded and moved inside, breathing a sigh of relief as the freshness caressed her face, soothing the redness.

The balcony was in full sun, so she moved to the desk inside. Tapping the pen against her front teeth, she searched for inspiration but words eluded her; her mind was too cluttered with images of Theo and echoes of his voice.

"Get a grip," she told herself as she began doodling flowers on a scrap of paper, her thoughts turning to the prospect of the evening ahead.

Chapter 10

Clothes littered the bed as Alice frantically tried to find a suitable outfit. In truth she had nothing appropriate to wear; she was expecting to just eat and write, not be having dinner with a curiously intriguing man.

The best look she could come up with was a pair of grey viscose wide-leg trousers, and a washed-out black t-shirt which hugged her breasts and accentuated every undulating curve of her torso. She blotted powder on her cheeks to mop up the shine, and daubed the same brown lipstick she always wore on her lips. She had worn her hair in a shoulder-length bob since childhood, with the exception of growing it slightly longer whilst at university. As a final flourish, she grabbed a strand of multi-coloured wooden beads and flung them around her neck.

As she closed her bedroom door, her mouth felt as dry as an English lawn at the height of summer. Hesitating in the corridor, she considered eating some of the biscuits she had brought from home instead of going down to dinner.

"Hello," said Zoe, appearing from her room in a cloud of sweet perfume.

"You look amazing," Alice said, wide-eyed, gazing at yet another skin-tight satin outfit.

"Just something I threw in the suitcase at the last minute; glad I did."

Alice was swept away by Zoe's aura, and before she knew it she was standing in the doorway of the dining room, where only Marlon was seated. Zoe swished past her, arriving at his table, and procuring a breadstick to nibble on.

Alice moved silently to a table by herself, tugging her t-shirt over her stomach, before resting her clammy hands in her lap.

Clive arrived, scanning the room before heading towards Zoe and

Marlon's table. Alice observed Zoe frown as she looked up at him, and Marlon just shuffled in his seat. Clive appeared oblivious to his ripple-effect, and took a seat.

Alice had just taken a large mouthful of wine when over the rim of her glass she saw Theo standing in the doorway. Suddenly, the wine in her mouth made her feel like she was drowning, making her struggle to swallow. She began choking. Bending down to retrieve a tissue from her handbag, she spluttered droplets of wine all over her hands. After wiping herself clean, she straightened up to find Theo standing over her.

"Are you okay?"

She nodded, even though she knew her face blotchy, and her clothes were dotted with tiny wet marks. She sensed all eyes staring at her, and her face glowed furiously. Maggie arrived as a form of distraction to take orders. Alice requested couscous with a mélange of meats, whilst Theo ordered fish and steamed rice.

"Shall I top up your wine, or have your swallowing reflexes abandoned you?"

"A top up would be perfect, thank you," she replied curtly. "And I'm more than capable of swallowing, but thank you for your concern."

"I'm sorry. Perhaps we should start again?"

She inclined her head. "I do embarrass easily."

"We all have our unwanted quirks."

Maggie placed bread and pâté on every table for people to tuck into whilst awaiting their main dish. Theo spread the pâté on thickly and tucked in.

"What do you make of that then?" Zoe said, casually rolling her eyes in Alice and Theo's direction.

"She's better suited to his age," replied Marlon. "Should stop him sniffing around you like a dog on heat."

"That's rather crude."

"You need someone a bit rough around the edges, not refined like that guy."

Zoe fluttered her eyelashes before taking a sip of wine.

"So, Marlon, how are you finding this retreat," asked Clive, patting his forehead with a handkerchief.

"Not as good as I'd hoped."

"Sorry to hear that. Aren't you going to ask about my writing?"

Marlon downed that last of the wine in his glass and instantly refilled it. "And what is it that you are writing, exactly?"

"A thriller, a catch-me-if-you-can type of thriller. The protagonist is gay."

"Sounds intriguing, what's the plotline?" enthused Zoe.

"I'm not ready to reveal it just yet. Don't you just love being teased?" he taunted.

"You sound like a master of suspense, I'm hooked already," she squealed.

Marlon was more interested in watching Theo and Alice, who appeared to be conversing more now that the wine was flowing.

At the next table along, Enid and Doris were excitedly talking about Agatha Christie films.

Marlon had lost his appetite.

"So, tell me more about yourself," Theo asked, brushing toast crumbs from the red-and-white-checked tablecloth.

"I've told you already my life's been rather uneventful. I only work part-time in a bakery, mainly because I've been caring for my mother who became disabled after a stroke." She paused to nibble on some toast.

"Sounds like you had little choice in your career, but what about your love life? A pretty woman like you must have had a few relationships." His toes curled in his loafers.

"It feels a bit bizarre talking to you about such things; I don't know you that well."

Theo smiled as he watched her toy with her wine glass. She lacked sophistication and her life echoed emptiness, but somehow she was going to make beguiling fodder for his daily column. He sensed she may be close to revealing a tragedy in her past that led her to the woman she had become.

The aroma of a spicy merguez and chunks of lamb mixed with couscous hung in the balmy evening air as Maggie flitted around the room, clearing plates before returning with the main meals. Theo looked enviously at Alice's plate, regretting his healthier option of fish. He still had Joanna's voice in his head taunting him about his expanding waistline.

"What would you have done if your mother wasn't ill?" Theo asked as he sliced into the white fish with the side of his fork.

"Archaeology always appealed to me. Finding hidden treasures from past civilizations would have been fascinating."

"Is it too late for that dream?"

"Of course it is," she replied tersely. She moved the food around her plate, sending plumes of steam towards her face. "Anyway, what do you do?"

"I'm a solicitor, nothing exciting though, I just deal with house sales."

"It's more interesting than my job. I'm surprised you're sitting with me, truth be told. I'd have thought Zoe was more your type."

"Do I look like a man with a *type*?"

"All men have a type. You're no different."

"You sound like a woman who's been hurt."

"You're very blunt." Scooping up some couscous, she forked it into her mouth, relapsing into silence with a furrowed brow.

"I must say," Clive said, "your job certainly gives you a great body." He let his gaze linger on Marlon as he picked up his wine glass. "I bet you have women clambering all over you."

"I don't have any problem in that area."

"I'm sure you don't," Zoe said softly. "But here, you only have me as an option."

"Maybe not," grinned Clive.

Maggie entered the room and began clearing away the plates. She noticed Marlon had hardly touched the meal. "Was the food not to your liking?"

"No, it's delicious; I'm not hungry, that's all."

"Hope that's nothing to do with me," said Clive.

Marlon pursed his lips and sat back in his chair, avoiding eye contact with anyone.

"How about some brie and grapes, or a lemon cheesecake? Anything suit you there, Marlon?" Maggie inquired.

"I'll have another carafe of wine, please. And do you have any whiskey?"

"I would have thought you'd treat your body like a temple," Maggie said.

"This is a retreat from everything, including my body."

Maggie smiled as she hurried away with a pile of plates.

She returned, placing a carafe of wine and a glass of whiskey in front of him. He proffered the wine to the others before filling his own glass. He then downed his whiskey in one swift gulp.

"You look like a troubled man," said Zoe.

"Show me a man without any troubles and I'll show you a liar and an addict," he replied quietly.

Chapter 11

Marlon staggered towards his room, clutching the whiskey bottle he had procured from Maggie. Zoe tried escorting him up, but he forcefully rebuffed her, saying he wanted to be alone.

Closing the door behind him, he exhaled, allowing his arms to flop by his sides so the bottle knocked against his thigh.

He walked towards the open window and out onto the balcony where he saw the older women sitting at a table drinking tea and chatting with Maggie. They had such simple lives, any troubles lost in the ether of their pasts.

Opening the bottle, he poured a large measure into a glass. Swirling the amber liquid he watched a vortex appear, wishing he could jump right in to be swallowed whole. To be lost forever.

Life used to be a sweet adventure for him. He had a dream job working with invariably attractive women on a one-to-one basis, and playing with them in his free time. But then he made a mistake, one mistake that had endless repercussions.

He continued flirting with women and making the right moves, but he went no further. He dare not.

Laughter from the garden jolted him from his psychic entanglement. Everyday sounds were magnified by the darkness that had descended without him noticing, and his emotions were intensified by the alcohol and introspection. Pain coursed through his body as though his blood was acid.

He poured another drink, taking brief refuge in the alcohol before guilt clouded his thoughts again. It was time to cease his endless circle of emotional torture. It was time.

The Wishful Woman

I shared a table at dinner time with the woman I've named Anna. She's not someone you'd notice in a crowded room, or even in an empty room, come to that. She has a façade of blandness, capable of blending in to a magnolia-coloured painted wall.

Some of you may feel that's a harsh description of a fellow human being, but I'm not here to play nice, I'm here to give you the insider view of a writing retreat, and those wannabes who attend.

Anna is the woman, if you remember, who's writing a romantic novel; who lives her life vicariously through her words. Her lack of experience probably leaps from every page, making her characters two-dimensional, and all suffering from the ubiquitous unrequited love. Yawn.

Anna's private life gives me very little to write about. However, it's what she doesn't say that may prove to be more fascinating. I believe there has been a love in her life in some form or another, and they hurt her badly. The hurt has coloured her view of life, the world, and men, so much so, she trusts no one and no longer believes in the concept of true love. Only in her novels does she allow her heart to be submerged by l'amour.

But how can someone be so weak? Everyone has suffered one trauma or another in their life, but they don't allow themselves to drown in self-pity and morose thoughts. Her mother died recently, but that's what happens to parents at some point in our lives. Plus she was her carer so her death, I imagine, has been a release in many ways.

The bizarre thing is I believe this woman is attracted to me. How conceited, I hear you cry. So what makes me claim this? She becomes shy and tongue-tied around me, her cheeks glow like beacons, and she only gives me fleeting eye contact. I catch her watching me when she thinks I'm not looking; she's pitiful in so many ways.

I'm not the least bit attracted to her, but I'm quite bored here, so I'll see how far she'll let me delve into her past, and who knows what else. Watch this space.

Theo pressed send then pondered what to do next. *Being abroad should be more fun than this*, he thought. His closed his laptop and headed downstairs, where he found Alice reading in the corner of the lounge.

"I'm surprised to find you here," he said.

She jumped, closing the book firmly. "I fancied a change of scenery." She shifted around in her chair, being careful not to catch his eye.

"What made you choose to write in the romance genre?" he asked, pulling over a chair.

"It's what I like to read. I like stories about relationships and the quintessential happy ending. I suppose that makes me sound pathetic?"

Theo was lapping it up. "Of course not. It makes you sound like a typical woman."

"That's stereotyping half the population. I didn't take you for a misogynist."

Theo laughed, throwing his head back. "My friends have many names for me, including that one." He caught Maggie's eye as she walked through the room. "Could we have two cappuccinos please?"

"I don't drink coffee this late at night."

"Live dangerously, Alice, you're in France."

She liked the way he said her name. It reminded her of the feel of velvet on her fingertips: soothing yet strong.

"In fact, why don't I cancel those coffees and let's take a stroll to the café I saw in the local village."

"You smell like you've been there already."

He ignored her comment. "Maggie, hold those drinks please, we're heading out."

Alice hesitated, then stood, leaving her book on the side table and gripping her handbag behind her back as they strolled silently down the dirt track towards the country lane.

Walking side by side down the narrow road, the backs of their hands lingered as they brushed against one another. Alice knew her face was scarlet and was comforted by the veil of navy darkness obscuring her, with only a smattering of stars piercing the canopy.

"The night is young, as they say," he said on reaching the café. "A table with the view of the stars. Perfect."

A young woman took their order as they sat down. A couple of portly French men sat at the adjacent table, drinking Pastis and smoking Gauloises.

"God, I love that smell," Theo said under his breath. His nostrils flaring as he inhaled deeply.

"Really? I find it really repugnant." She wrinkled her nose.

"Excuse me a minute," he said, getting up and wandering into the building.

The young woman brought out their drinks, and Alice mumbled *merci* in an attempt to show solidarity. The woman smiled stiffly.

Returning to the table, Theo ripped open a packet of cigarettes, removed one, and stuck it between his lips. Alice watched, perplexed, as he struck a match and ignited it. He took a deep drag and exhaled the noxious fumes into the air, obliterating the stars for a few seconds.

"I didn't know you smoked?"

"I used to, but I gave up. I haven't smoked for three years." Again he inhaled deeply and attempted to blow smoke-rings, but only managing to produce dirty-looking clouds.

"Why start again now?"

"Why not?"

Alice held her wine glass under her nose. He looked a natural smoker, whereas she suspected she would look gauche with a cigarette between her lips.

"You must have done something rebellious in your youth," he said, letting smoke swirl from his mouth like dragon's breath.

"What do you class as rebellious?"

"Oh come on, I mean things like smoking, taking drugs, threesomes, orgies, shoplifting, tattoos. There are endless ways to be rebellious."

Alice took a sip of drink and kept the liquid in her mouth before swallowing hard with an audible gulp. The fingers of her left hand drummed on the table as she sifted through memories. "I'm sorry to disappoint you, but the only drug I've tried is alcohol. I've told you before, I'm boring."

"How old are you Alice? Forty-six?"

"Forty-four actually," she replied brusquely.

"What's a couple of years?"

"In the wrong direction."

"Okay, okay. Still, you must have at least one skeleton in the closet."

"What's it to you? Why are you so interested in my past?"

Theo stubbed out his cigarette in the ashtray and watched the last breaths of smoke drift into the night. "Call it a writer's curiosity, don't you have it? All right, why don't I tell you something about me?"

Alice sat up and inclined her head in his direction, relaxing at the reprieve of her own interrogation.

"I'm recently divorced and my twenty-one-year-old son hasn't spoken to me for four years after a gargantuan row." He paused for a large mouthful of wine, before pulling out another cigarette.

Alice wished she had not worn the bangles on her wrist which jangled and clunked every time she picked up her drink.

"I suppose divorce isn't rebellious these days. Most of our friends have been down that route. Perhaps my skeleton is clothed in the fabric of my relationship with Justin."

"You're quite poetic when you talk."

"That's the writer in me," he smiled.

"Are you hoping to rekindle your relationship with him?"

"I'm not sure what I want anymore. Perhaps he's better off without me."

"How could you think that? Family's forever."

"Nothing is forever, Alice. Only a child would have that sugar-coated innocence about them, and you're no child."

"Are you back to my age again?"

"You seem fixated with your age. Does it bother you?"

"Age wasn't an issue up until forty-one, but now I'm hurtling towards mid-to-late-forties, I can see the crevices in my face appearing as each day passes. These aren't highlights in my hair, but streaks of white," she said, holding up a few tresses.

Theo ordered more drinks then settled back into the metal chair, shifting around in the unyielding frame.

"Do you want to try a smoke?" he asked, thrusting the packet towards her.

With all the wine she had imbued since dinner, she paused. "No, it would be a stupid thing to do."

"I saw you considered it. Go on take a couple of puffs, live a little."

"That's exactly what smokers do; they live only a little."

"Very droll," he said before lighting one. He drew on it hard before puffing out the smoke, maintaining constant eye contact.

"Oh, what the heck," she muttered, taking the cigarette from his hand. She faltered and held it to her lips. As the smoke engulfed her mouth and ripped at the back of her throat, she coughed and spluttered, much to his amusement.

Alice grabbed her glass, gulping down some wine to extinguish the disgusting taste. "Oh my God, why do people do that?" she cried. "It's foul."

Her exclamations attracted the attention of the two men at the other table, and Theo's raucous laughter only added to their curiosity.

"You give up too easily, give it another go," he urged.

"Absolutely not," she said croakily, handing it back.

He shrugged, noticing the faint brown lipstick stain around the rim before he stuck it in his mouth.

Alice drank quickly to relieve her dusty mouth, watching him carefully. He looked weary with an edge of melancholy.

"I think there's more going on in your head than you care to admit. They say divorce is stressful."

He smiled wryly, tapping the spent ash from the end of his cigarette onto the floor. He rolled the diminishing stick between his fingers as he reflected on what to say. "I sometimes wish I'd done more adventurous things in my life, and I suppose I don't want you to feel the same in years to come."

"Is that why you're coercing me into smoking and drinking too much?"

"Maybe. Or maybe it's because I know you won't sleep with me unless your inhibitions are dampened."

Alice's mouth dropped open as her eyebrows lifted to meet her hairline. She wiped her clammy hands on her dress. "So you think I'll sleep with you if I'm drunk enough. Is this why you brought me here?" She strained to keep her tone level.

"Not at first, but now . . . my feelings have taken a turn."

"Probably the alcohol?"

"Don't you think it could be you that's changed my view?"

"I doubt that very much. I'm not a nubile twenty-year-old with luscious waist-length hair and thighs with a vice grip."

Theo laughed, rocking his head backwards, sloshing wine from the glass he was holding. "Is that what you think men my age want?"

"That's what *all* men want. They want a cake they can eat, own, and put on show. Younger women are a status symbol for men like you. I saw the way you looked at the woman serving us."

"A man can appreciate beauty from afar; it doesn't mean he wants to roll around the bed with her all night."

Alice shuddered. "We should be heading back or I won't be able to get up to write in the morning." Feeling herself sway, she grabbed her bag and clutched it against her stomach.

When he went inside to pay, her thoughts drifted rudderless around her mind. The closer she pulled her bag towards her, the more she felt a part of her yearn to be touched to prove she was, on some level, an attractive woman.

But echoes of ugly memories raised their voices, battering her self-esteem, and drowning out the timid voice urging her to step outside the box. No amount of alcohol could obliterate those toe-curling memories, and by the time he returned, she had recoiled into the safety of her spinster-like shell.

Theo wrenched her arm off her bag and linked it through his before leading her back to the chateaux. An eerily electric silence connected them, and Alice wondered whether she would have the courage to let him get to know her more.

Chapter 12

Marlon lay sprawled out on his double bed as though his limbs were tied to the four posts. Above him, a white muslin canopy with tiny dark shadows of dead moths and flies hung over him like a shroud.

The chateau was quiet, and yet the silence was deafening. He stuffed his head under the pillow, realising he had nowhere left to turn as jagged edges of pain ripped through his mind leaving raw gaping slices of agonising imagery.

Rolling over, he dragged his bag out from under the bed, and pulled the zipper to reveal a jumble of t-shirts and boxers. Rifling around, he retrieved a bottle of anti-depressants, placing it on the bedside cabinet.

He remembered the day the doctor prescribed them.

"There's nothing to be ashamed of," he said. "Depression hits everyone at one time or another. I'll prescribe these for a short period whilst you undertake some counselling." The doctor was kind, but matter-of-fact.

To outsiders, Marlon gave the impression of having everything a young man could desire, including a string of stunning girlfriends, and a convertible Mercedes.

However, he had grown up in a God-fearing family who attended church every Sunday. His mother was suffocating, and his father had a rigid set of principals which he expected all his children to adhere to.

Marlon knew his father had been a player in his youth, before marrying his mother. He had inherited his father's good looks and luck with women. But with good looks came a curse. Expectations ran high and the inherent ideology that he would continue the line of good-looking boys was pressed into each layer of his soul.

When his parents returned to South Africa, they left him with the explicit hope that the next time they saw him, he would be engaged.

Living without their constant vigilance gave him the freedom to express himself in a way his parents would never have accepted. He loved being in the presence of beautiful women, but he had the freedom to notice that he was also intensely attracted to men.

He remembered desiring boys when he was at secondary school, but he thought it was his mind experimenting with his newly aroused hormones. However, the yearning persisted and was made worse by sports sessions at school.

As he thought about the naked, taut adolescent chests in the changing rooms, he broke out into a familiar sweat. When the boys took communal showers, he felt his throat constrict, and at night in his bedroom, he would fantasize about being with one of them under a stream of water.

He propped himself up on his elbows as his father's face, etched with disgust, floated in front of his eyes. Sitting up fully, he rubbed his eyes with his fists, willing the image to be expunged before reaching out for the bottle and pouring a large whiskey, downing it in one go. His instinct was to stop drinking, but he needed to numb the over-riding sensations of loathing and lust. There was no turning back.

His thought's turned to one particular evening, when he ventured into Soho in London and strolled around the cobbled streets filled with gay bars and sex shops. He was fascinated by the freedom gay couples were awarded, and without paying attention he wandered into a bustling bar where he met Clive Morris, and his fate was sealed.

He poured himself another drink and threw a handful of tablets in his mouth. He washed them down before picking up a pen and pad to write a letter to his parents, trying to explain the torturous life he had experienced since adolescence. *Please don't hate me.*

He poured himself another glass of alcohol and flushed down another handful of tablets, waiting for the hazy feeling to take over, allowing him to accomplish his final act.

A while later, with no whiskey or tablets left, he retrieved a piece of rope he had found in one of the chateaux's derelict outhouses, before hazily looking around the room to check it was tidy then slipping into the night.

The air was still as he walked towards the cluster of trees on the boundary of the chateaux's land, where he found a sturdy olive tree. Shinning clumsily up the gnarly trunk and grazing his knees, he inched out onto a thick branch, and firmly tied one end of the rope to it before slipping the noose around his neck.

Pausing to gaze up at the diamante, inky sky, he smiled, before rolling off the branch. The last sounds he heard were the cicadas and the creaking of the tautening rope.

Chapter 13

Painfully aware of his single bed, Theo decided to accompany Alice to her bedroom in the hope she had something more accommodating.

The corridor was dimly lit and the atmosphere tinged with the lingering scent of garlic. As they reached her bedroom door, he pressed her against it and covered her mouth with his. She stood still, arms dangling by her sides, mouth immobile.

He moved his mouth to her ear. "Key."

She fumbled in her bag which was wedged between them, then wiggled her way around to unlock the door.

The bed was covered in discarded clothes and pots of makeup. She saw a flash of disappointment in his eyes, and the light she had so rashly ignited was rapidly dimming.

Like a pair of university students, they crashed onto the bed, brushing the discarded items onto the floor. Theo began adeptly removing her clothing, but it was a different matter for her. She was entering an arena she had only visited once in the distant past, and she was feeling increasingly unsure of herself, as past voices echoed in her head.

Theo pulled away. "Is there something wrong?"

"I . . . I haven't done . . . this for a while."

He sat up straight. "Is this too quick?"

"Possibly. We hardly know one another."

"But the connection is definitely there, don't you think? And we are in France."

"What difference does that make?"

"Why come all this way and not be swept away by the French attitude to love?"

Her overwhelming emotion was the need to feel wanted, and he could potentially fulfil that desire. She was tired of living with regrets, and maybe the bitterness of her past would be expunged by this act?

As they both lay naked together, he looked into her eyes and she smiled in response. As he wrapped his arms around her, she was surprised his flesh was not as firm as she thought it would be, but found it helped her feel less anxious about her own squidgy proportions.

So this is what it feels like.

On entering the dining room, Alice spied Enid and Doris eating their breakfast. As they greeted each other, Alice thought if she smiled for much longer, her facial muscles would go into spasm.

As she took a seat at an empty table, Clive entered the room.

"*Bonjour*, dear lady, and how does this morning find you?" he said, gesturing to a chair at her table. "Gracious, your face belies secrets of the night, if I'm not mistaken."

Alice blushed furiously, putting her hand on her cheek. She was about to sweep away his remark when Zoe wandered over to their table, bringing with her a new scent of passionflower.

"You both look conspiratorial," she said, pulling out a chair.

"I was just saying Alice has a certain glow about her this morning," Clive said, giving her a wink.

"Unless she found a man wandering the garden, I fail to see who with," Zoe mused.

"I *am* sitting here," Alice protested, as Maggie approached the table with a large pot of coffee.

She took their orders and disappeared to the kitchen, almost bumping into Theo in the doorway. On seeing him, Alice averted her eyes and picked up the coffee pot. Theo nodded to the table then wandered out to the patio and sat at a table for one. Alice's heart plummeted to her stomach, leaving her feeling queasy and light-headed.

"I love the silent, moody type," Zoe said, tracing around the top of a glass with her finger.

Maggie arrived with a basket of warm croissants. Alice proceeded to rip a piece off and stuff it in her mouth as she watched the two older women move outside for their regular constitutional along the perimeter of the garden. She wished she was outside too, as she could only see the back of Theo's head and she wondered whether his face also betrayed him to the others; perhaps that was why he did not join them. Or perhaps he was ashamed he had sullied himself by sleeping with her.

She drained her cup and decided to start her writing session, when a piercing scream emanated from the garden. Theo was on his feet, shielding his eyes from the morning glare, as the two women scurried back towards the chateaux. Enid's face was crumpled into a mass of furrows; she was clearly sobbing, whilst stifling her screams with her hand.

"My God, what's happened?" exclaimed Maggie as she ran towards them.

Enid was inconsolable, her face drenched in tears and her hand still clamped over her mouth. Both women were visibly shaking, but Doris managed to relay what they had discovered in the boundary trees.

Maggie screeched for her husband, as Alice and Clive guided the women to some seats in the shade. They watched as Maggie, Marcus, and Theo hurriedly moved away, whilst Marcus talked rapidly in French on his mobile phone.

"Oh, poor Marlon, whatever possessed him to do that?" whispered Enid, finally. "He didn't appear to be a troubled man."

"We all have troubles to one extent or another," said Zoe, standing still in the direction of the tree, "but it takes damn courage to do that."

Alice squeezed Zoe's arm and shook her head as Enid let out another wail. Clive suggested someone make a large pot of tea, looking pointedly at Zoe, who took the cue and begrudgingly walked back inside, surreptitiously wiping a tear from her eye.

"You're quiet," Alice said under her breath to a pale-faced Clive. "What should we do now?"

"Be very British, and have a hot sweet tea. We're all in shock."

"I can't believe this has happened. Why do you think he did it?"

Clive shrugged, blotting his forehead with a powder-blue handkerchief. "We all have secrets," he whispered.

After the police had worked the scene, and Marlon's lifeless body was removed, everyone sat around the lounge in thick-edged silence. No one moved, and no one dared look at one another.

"I wonder if they'll let us know what happened," Zoe said finally.

"The police will want to interview us all individually first. They strongly suspect suicide, but won't be certain until after the autopsy," Marcus replied, in a reedy voice. "No one will ever want to stay here again, apart perhaps from morbid gawkers."

Maggie thrust her elbow into his ribs. Her glare sent him fleeing to the kitchen to wallow in the mire of present hell and future failure.

"Truth is like sand," Doris said quietly. "You can hold on to it tightly, but it will always find its way out."

Clive shuddered. "Do you think we could have a shot of whiskey, or whatever? For medicinal purposes only, you understand."

Maggie obliged, fetching a bottle and eight shot glasses. She poured a measure in each glass before handing them around.

"You're not supposed to drink alcohol when in shock, it lowers you blood pressure," said Zoe.

"I'm sure we'll cope," said Maggie before tipping back her head and throwing the liquid down her throat. She sensed Marcus watching her from the doorway as she poured herself another drink.

Alice felt slightly hungover from the night before, but it felt like an unspoken toast to Marlon, so she sipped hers whilst trying not to cough as it caught the back of her throat.

A policeman entered the room with a letter in an evidence bag. Clive spied the paper and felt the blood drain from his head. The policeman made it clear, in English with a heavy French accent, that they would shortly be spoken to, but that there was nothing to fear, as the coroner was almost certain it was suicide.

Marcus returned to sit next to his wife. He slumped forwards and put his head in his hands. "We're ruined," he uttered. "Absolutely ruined."

Maggie rolled her eyes.

Chapter 14

The remainder of the retreat was a complete washout where writing was concerned. Even crime writer Enid could not rekindle her word flow following the gruesome discovery. The image of Marlon's hanging body was imprinted on both the women's minds, so they returned home to England after being interviewed by the police.

Clive had segregated himself from the group, preferring to take a bottle of wine to his room. He had nothing to do; he wasn't a writer, and had no intention of being one. His role had simply been that of a stalker. "I literally stalked a man to death," he mumbled to himself, and to the ghost of Marlon he sensed prowling around.

"So you two, what are your plans for this evening, seeing as we're the only three sociable guests?" said Zoe, prodding the ice cubes in her gin and tonic.

"I would suggest we trundle down to the bar in the village, but I fear Maggie will feel abandoned. Her husband appears to be permanently pissed," replied Theo.

"So why don't we stay here and get pissed too. I write better erotica when I'm hammered." Zoe gazed at Theo from under her thick lashes.

"Good idea. However, inspiration has just hit me, so I must write. I'll catch up with you ladies later."

Sex and Suicide

I hope the title has caught your attention, readers, as this truly is a bumpy ride. Perhaps the title gives too much away?

I took the spinsterish Anna to the local bar where I tried to find out more about her. What I did find out was that she can't hold her drink which makes her very easy to lure into bed (with her consent, you understand).

It wouldn't surprise you to learn that we had sex in the dark, doubtlessly to hide her lumps, bumps, and possible varicose veins. But even the dark couldn't absolve the awkwardness. It was a fumble akin to the back row grope I did as a fifteen-year-old with my first girlfriend in the cinema. Anna was clumsy, stilted, a bit rough at times (not in the right way), and grossly inept at being in-tune with her own body—let alone mine.

The session was quick; I wanted it that way.

But in juxtaposition, whilst we were delving into Anna's unknown sexual and emotional territory, a fellow wannabe author was hanging himself from an olive tree in the grounds. Yes, you read that correctly, we had a suicide in the camp.

This writing retreat has turned out more newsworthy than even I'd anticipated. Who'd have thought that sex and suicide would be two elements of this week? I can't imagine it getting more exciting than this, although young Zara is still giving me her come-to-bed eyes, who can blame her?

Who knows what tomorrow's column will bring?

After pressing SEND, he got up and poured himself a whiskey. He caught sight of himself in the mirror, and pulled in his stomach. He brushed his hand over his hair, worrying he could see more grey before remembering a night in London when a woman told him he looked deliciously distinguished. He smiled at his reflection.

A tap at his door found him face to face with Alice; his smile faded slightly.

"Am I bothering you? I mean, have you finished writing?"

"Do you want to come in?" He stepped aside to let her pass.

"I don't know how you can write at a time like this? I can't shake off the shock of it all. I keep thinking I'll see Marlon in the dining room, or on the terrace."

Theo poured her a glass of whiskey and handed it to her as she perched on the edge of his bed. She took a sip, finding she was beginning to get accustomed to the heat and throttle of neat alcohol. "Can I see some of your writing?"

"I don't show it to anyone until the final copy, I'm afraid."

"I won't criticize you; I'm hardly an accomplished writer."

"What should the three of us do this evening?" he asked, deflecting her persistence.

Alice took a sip of drink, searching the ceiling with her eyes. "You mean the pair of us and Zoe? She just wants to get drunk. She's troubled by Marlon's death; I think they got on well."

"I think she gets on well with any man."

"I suppose you mean you like her in that way too."

"What way is that?"

Alice downed her whiskey and coughed a little. "You find her sexy. It wouldn't surprise me if you did."

"I appreciate the view, but she's rather too young for me."

"But you wouldn't say no."

"What's this obsession with me and other women, all of a sudden? You're not jealous and possessive after last night, are you?"

Alice stood up and poured herself another drink. "That would imply I have some vested interest or ownership." She held the bottle over his glass and poured when he nodded. "And I'm not sure I fit in with either category."

"So that's settled, let's do something with Zoe."

"And what about Clive? He seems to have taken Marlon's death very hard."

"I think he had a little man-crush on Marlon, with his tight chest and sultry eyes."

"Sounds like you had your own man-crush going on," she laughed quietly.

Theo frowned and suggested they head back downstairs. Arm in arm, they entered the dining room, and found they were the first ones to arrive. Maggie, relieved at having company, rushed over with a carafe of local red wine and the menu.

"Is Clive coming down?" she asked, pouring the wine.

"We haven't seen him, but I'm sure hunger will drive him down eventually," replied Theo.

Maggie's face was pale underneath her suntan, and her demeanour more defeated than proud. Marcus had not materialized since the police had left, preferring solitude with a bottle of wine in one hand and a glass in the other. Maggie feared they would soon be out of wine between Marcus's and Clive's new habit.

As Theo and Alice ordered onion soup followed by Steak au Poivre, Zoe arrived, shortly followed by Clive, his face blotchy and stippled with bristles.

"Things feel slightly more normal when you're all here. Such a pity the two old dears chose to go home," Maggie said, pouring Clive some wine.

She returned to the kitchen and found Marcus hunched over the kitchen table.

"If we don't start attracting more guests, we won't be able to pay the bills. We're sinking in quagmire."

"Oh Marcus, this is just a blip. All the wine you're drinking isn't helping our profit margin."

Marcus groaned as his thoughts drifted back to what they once had when they were still living in England.

His career as a city trader had provided them with a very comfortable life. They lived in a five bedroom detached house in Buckinghamshire, and their lifestyle was both decadent and fast paced. And it was the latter he objected to.

He would commute to Canary Wharf in London, and sometimes stay in their London flat if he had to wine and dine clients. The work was exhausting yet exhilarating, but he was beginning to feel his life was a blur, and he was not seeing enough of his wife. So when the opportunity of redundancy appeared above the parapet, he grabbed it with both hands.

Maggie was delighted at the prospect of seeing more of him, and was equally pleased about his redundancy package, which she believed would keep them both very comfortable whilst he carry out occasional work as a consultant.

They both knew early on in their relationship that neither of them wanted children, and those sentiments never wavered. Their honesty with one another forged a strong bond between them.

Never in their twelve years together had he uttered a desire to leave their homeland and move abroad. And he had also never suggested Maggie work for a living. Her role was to be a supportive wife, a dazzling dinner guest at functions, and a scintillating hostess, holding soirees for when Marcus had to entertain clients. She fulfilled her role admirably even though she found many of the female guests vacuous and elliptical.

Then one day, he arrived home with two tickets to Bordeaux in the Aquitaine region of southwest France. Maggie envisaged horse riding around vineyards, strolls along sandy beaches, and meals in exquisite restaurants dotted along the port. So she packed accordingly.

When they arrived by taxi in a village just outside Bordeaux, she was surprised to find they were sleeping in room above a café. There were no swanky restaurants to delight their palates with Michelin star food, or extravagant shops where he could purchase her more diamond jewellery to signify his unyielding devotion.

After a less than comfortable night's sleep and a breakfast consisting of coffee so strong you could almost stand a spoon in it, he took her on a short stroll to a chateaux.

Maggie waited to hear the history attached to the dilapidated building, as he had always had a passion for history and historical buildings in general. Then gradually it dawned on her. The once dapper city trader was talking about renovating the chateaux to its former glory and running it as a guest house. A lump formed in her throat as the idea swilled around her head.

"You want us to run a guest house? Who would do the cooking, the cleaning, and changing all the beds?"

"We would. We'd divide up the chores and have a rota so we didn't get complacent. I've a vision of running a retreat for harassed Londoners. We'd offer tranquillity, good food and wine, plus excellent rooms and service. What could go wrong?"

Maggie shoulder's sagged. *Where to start*, she thought to herself.

The occupants of the chateaux greeted them like long-lost relatives. They chattered along quickly in French, most of which Marcus understood, but Maggie's school-girl French was rather rusty. Nothing made sense to her. She wanted a gin and tonic to dull her mounting panic.

The chateaux was beautiful in a shabby-chic sort of way, and Maggie could see it had potential for a young couple heavily into DIY. It also came with a few acres of land where mimosa and olive trees dappled the ground in the sunlight. Surrounding the land were vineyards with a rosebush at the end of each row. Marcus informed her that they were planted in order to detect the early signs of mildew fungus disease before it savaged the vines. Swathes of woody lavender bushes filled the front garden.

"How many other places to view are you going to surprise me with whilst we're here?" she asked.

"None, this is the only one."

"It's a long way to come to see only one place. You could have checked out more online."

"I did, and this was the only suitable one."

Maggie turned to face him, her eyes narrowed. "How long have you been doing this behind my back?"

"Long enough to know when the right one turns up."

Maggie began to see little red dots in front of her eyes, and her breathing became shallow. "Don't tell me you're thinking of putting an offer in on this place."

"No . . ."

"Thank God," she interjected. "I—"

She was interrupted by the owner of the place walking towards them with a bottle of Champagne in his hands, whilst his wife carried crystal flutes on an ornate tarnished silver tray.

"*Santé*," cried out the French couple, as they held their glasses aloft.

Marcus reciprocated, whilst Maggie watched the scene with clarity dawning. "What are we celebrating? You haven't actually put an offer in have you?" she hissed through gritted teeth.

"We're a bit further down the line than that. We're calling in at the solicitors after this to sign the paperwork. This will be ours at the end of the day."

Maggie nearly choked on her drink, her eyes watering as the bubbles rose up her nose. Marcus saw the signs and guided her to a chair before she crumpled into it.

"Perhaps I should have told you, but I thought I'd surprise you instead. Wrong choice?"

"How is this going to work? Are we splitting our time between England and France?"

"Not exactly. Let's finish this and have a chat over lunch."

Maggie was never one for causing a scene, so she duly quaffed her drink. They all kissed each other on the cheeks before walking back down the sweeping drive, fine particles of dust coating Maggie's lips and eyelashes. He reached out for her hand, but she clenched her fist and pulled it away.

Her facial muscles ached with the forced smiles she had maintained for the last hour and a half. "I can't eat; my stomach's in knots. What have you done, Marcus?"

"I've bought us a slice of the idyllic lifestyle we were seeking. More clement weather and a laid back approach to life which will suit us both."

"And you've done this without consulting me? I thought we had no secrets from one another."

"This wasn't a secret like gambling or cross-dressing; it's a beautiful gift of a new life for us."

"I realize that, but I loved our life as it was. I love England, our home, our families, our friends . . ."

"We're not moving to Australia, it's only across the English Channel. We can still visit them and they can come and stay here, there'll be enough room."

Maggie linked her arm through his, pulling him closer. "I do love you. It's just come as a big shock, that's all." She turned to face him. "It'll be fun," she smiled.

Little did they know.

Chapter 15

"It seems ridiculous we have to crush together in a single bed when we know there's a four-poster double in the room next to mine," said Theo, fidgeting next to her.

"That's gross. We couldn't possibly use his room."

"Why not? He's not using it. I could ask Maggie."

"Then they'll all know."

"And you think they haven't already guessed?"

"I don't like to think about it. This is a writers' retreat not a singles hotel."

"Are you embarrassed about me?"

Alice blushed, burying her head in his chest. "I'm embarrassed that people know I'm having sex." Her voice trailed off to a whisper.

"That's pathetic. I imagine Maggie and Marcus have done it during our stay."

Alice squealed with her mouth closed, slapping his chest with the palm of her hand. She pulled at the sheet, wrapping it around her as she climbed out of bed, finding the floor pleasantly cool underfoot.

Behind her, she could hear Theo pulling up his trousers and slipping on his loafers.

He moved behind her and wrapped his arms around her body. "I'll catch up with you later." He kissed her on the top of her head before leaving the room.

Alice relaxed as she heard the door close behind her. Making love with Theo had become a regular occurrence and she had become accustomed to wanting his touch, but she still had residual anxiety about the aftermath.

Water thudded on the top of her head as she stood in the shower, letting the accumulated sweat roll away towards the plughole. Soaping her body, she remembered Theo's fingers travelling the same route, exploring the curves and arches of her naked, ample flesh. She closed her eyes, remembering the smell of his body as it lay close to her.

Once in her room, still wrapped in a towel, she moved to her writing desk, hoping inspiration would strike. But instead, she glanced out of her window and caught sight of the clump of trees where Marlon's body was found. Whilst she was experiencing new feelings for Theo, Marlon was hanging himself to rid himself of every emotion residing within him. Sex was the instigator of shame, hate, and disgust for many.

Of course that was life, she mused. People die as someone is being born; people are receiving donated organs as a soldier loses a limb in a mortar attack. She just wished Marlon had not chosen the retreat as the time to go.

But she had another worry: love. The last time she fell in love was such a painful time, she had all but obliterated it from the recesses of her mind. But glimpses of the pain were returning, and it was that which was standing in her way of writing and living.

By the time Alice adjourned to the patio, she found Theo in deep conversation with Zoe, who had her hand on his thigh. Alice controlled her urge to run back inside, forcing herself to walk towards the pair.

"Hello, Alice," cooed Zoe, "did you have a productive writing session?"

Alice nodded, fearing that if she spoke her high pitch would expose the strain she was feeling. She hovered by the table as though requiring permission to sit down, rather than commanding her presence as the woman who had just slept with the only male at the table just a few hours earlier.

"I was telling Theo how bored I get in the evenings when you two disappear. Where do you get to, by the way?" Zoe asked, smiling.

Alice wanted to jealously guard their secret escape but Theo had no such concern.

"A run-down but quaint bar in the local village. What have you been doing?"

"When Marlon was around, I was totally entertained. But after, you know . . . I've been abandoned. Even Clive's deserted me. So, are we going to that bar tonight?"

Please say no, Alice thought to herself, only to hear Theo extend an invitation to her. Defeated, Alice took a seat and waited for Maggie to take her order.

The aroma of fennel and fish engulfed the kitchen as Maggie prepared the evening meal, whilst Marcus poured over the accounts at the kitchen table, assisted by a bottle of red wine.

Zoe walked over to where Alice and Theo were sitting. "Can I join you both for dinner?"

"Sure," replied Theo, patting the seat next to him.

Alice watched warily as Zoe flicked her glossy hair over her shoulder. She smouldered as she poured herself a glass of wine, letting her lips part softly to display just a hint of her white teeth. Theo responded by lifting the corners of his mouth.

"Alice and I were discussing staying on a couple of days longer. Neither of us has to get back just yet. What about you?"

Alice crossed her fingers in her lap and held her breath.

"You're so lucky, I've got to get back for work. So, are you two staying on for writing purposes, or something else?" she grinned.

Alice shuffled in her seat, picking up her wine glass. "I didn't get as much writing done as I'd hoped," she murmured before taking a large sip.

Zoe laughed. "You're a hopeless liar. I only have to look at the pair of you to see what's been going on."

"What can I say? I'm electric," replied Theo with a wink.

Alice screwed her eyes shut, wincing at his peacocking.

Clive crept into the dining room and after a bit of coercion, sat with them for dinner. Maggie brought over another bottle of wine and gave Clive a sympathetic smile, noticing his red-rimmed eyes.

"Marlon's death appears to have affected you badly," said Theo. "I didn't realize you knew him that well."

All eyes focused on Clive as he poured a glass of wine before knocking most of it back in a couple of gulps.

"It's a long story and not one I'm prepared to share," he mumbled.

"So you did know him," Zoe replied. "Why didn't either of you mention it?"

"Because Marlon was ashamed of having sex with me," Theo stated.

A gasp splintered across the group.

"But Marlon wasn't gay, he couldn't keep his hands off me," shrieked Zoe.

"I think you might find our friend was bi-sexual," replied Theo.

"You're not saying he killed himself because of that, surely?" asked Alice, finding her voice.

"Maybe he couldn't risk the shame on his family? What do you think?" Theo said, turning to Clive.

The thread veins on Clive's cheeks glowed as he poured himself another drink, his hand visibly shaking, sloshing wine on the table. "I know what you're all thinking, but Theo's got it wrong. I never harmed him . . ."

"But you followed him here, don't deny it," Theo said firmly.

"Who do you think you are? Bloody Poirot?"

"I've been watching you over the course of the week. Your interactions with Marlon told me a lot about you both. The shifty looks, the quiet but intense conversations when you thought no one was around."

"You were spying on us?" Clive raised his voice, attracting Maggie's attention.

"Everything all right in here?" she asked, popping her head around the door.

"Theo's explaining why Marlon topped himself," replied Zoe. "Do continue, this is fascinating."

"I've nothing more to say," shouted Clive, jumping to his feet and swiping the bottle from the table. He looked at each person in turn before scurrying to his room.

"You shouldn't goad him like that, you can see he's upset," Alice said disapprovingly.

"Just his drama queen tendencies," grunted Theo.

"I think you're quite clever, Theo," Zoe purred, arching her back as she sat in the chair.

Alice glared at her from behind her wine glass. "The poor man's suffering. You shouldn't be toying with his emotions."

"If only we knew what his suicide note said. The police wouldn't tell us," said Zoe, completely ignoring Alice.

"The police wouldn't have given us all permission to go home if anyone was implicated." Theo sat back in his chair, looking between the women before his eyes rested on Zoe's face.

Maggie emerged from the kitchen, and everyone turned to her expectantly.

"He left it for his parents," she whispered.

"Did you see what it said?" Zoe said eagerly.

Maggie scoured the room before stepping closer to the table. "The police asked Marcus to translate it for them."

"And?"

"Theo's on the right lines. Marlon is—was—bi-sexual, but couldn't come to terms with his sexuality. He seemed racked with remorse about his recent behaviour."

"What, sleeping with Zoe," laughed Theo.

"Cheeky bugger," she said, slapping his arm. "Anyway, we never actually slept together, not like you and Alice."

Alice covered her face with her hands as Theo roared with laughter.

"This has been a disastrous retreat. I'm sure none of you are further on with your novels." A heavy sigh punctuated Maggie's sentiment.

"I'm still writing daily," boasted Theo.

"You're all heart," muttered Alice.

"To conclude what I was saying," continued Maggie, "Clive's name wasn't mentioned, so perhaps you should go easy on him."

"Okay, just to please you, I'll lay off him, but he needs to buck up, he's polluting the atmosphere," conceded Theo.

With a loud exhale, Alice excused herself from the table; all the talk of death had clawed at her wounds.

Her room felt claustrophobic so she parted the muslin curtains and stood on the balcony, forcing herself to take in the view as she visualized Marlon's spirit roaming the grounds. Shuddering, she returned inside, when there was a knock at her door.

"I was wondering if we could cancel going out tonight, I've got a blinding headache. I'm going to bed," Theo said faintly.

As he walked away, she found herself partly relieved yet missing him, even though he was not truly hers to miss.

Picking up her diary, a photo of her mother fell to the floor instantly transporting her back to London, to the noisy flat and the smell of lavender. Her time there seemed a lifetime away, yet it was within touching distance once more. She allowed a solitary tear to edge down her cheek and drop from her chin.

Chapter 16

Bye, Bye, Bi

So we finally discover that Mark killed himself because he was ashamed of being bi-sexual. What a weak excuse to extinguish one's own life. The whole retreat has been reduced to a depressing wake in honour of a man we hardly knew. Well, most of us. It transpired that Colin had some knowledge of the deceased, although he was reluctant to divulge the extent of their friendship at first, but one only has to look at his monochrome handkerchiefs to be on the right path, which he then clarified.

I imagine you're also waiting to hear my developments with Anna. As you know, she is not a knowledgeable woman under the covers. Unfortunately, she doesn't fall into the category of the quiet ones are the dirty ones. *She's just a quiet one.*

Occasionally, I see glimpses into her inner self, as though her secret is getting harder to contain. I feel I will soon be able to reveal what she is trying to hide from the world. Let's hope it's worth it.

However, dear reader, I think she may be falling for me. I'm undoubtedly the most charismatic man she's ever met, but she's no more special to me than those that went before her, and those yet to come.

It occurred to me that Mark's death coincided with the la petite mort *experienced by Anna—possibly her first? That's one hell of a juxtaposition.*

He sat back, exhaling loudly, rubbing his temples as the echo of the headache remained. A battered packet of cigarettes caught his eye. Grabbing it, he shoved it in his pocket before heading down to the patio.

Maggie was serving Alice and Zoe their breakfasts, and Clive was sitting on the patio drinking coffee, staring into the middle-distance. Theo was not sure he was up to conversation, so he nodded at the women as he strode out to the patio and took a seat at the table adjacent to Clive.

"Another beautiful day," Theo ventured.

"I'm getting bored of the brightness; I'm missing the British gloom."

"You're going home shortly."

"Yes indeed. I have Truffles to keep me company."

"Truffles?"

"My Persian cat. My friend cares for her whilst I'm away."

Maggie brought Theo his usual coffee and two croissants to the table. "Sleep well?" she asked him.

"As always," he lied.

Theo watched Clive through his peripheral vision, his journalistic instinct urging him on.

"Do you want to talk about you and Marlon?"

Clive rubbed his chin and pursed his lips.

Theo slowly broke off a chunk of croissant then dipped it into his coffee before popping it into his mouth and devouring it quickly.

"What are you afraid of?"

"Of looking like an old fool. But I've been an old fool, haven't I?"

"Maybe, but I only guessed half of your story. Why don't you tell me just how much of a fool you've been?" Theo replied as he moved his chair so he was facing Clive.

"Are you a priest awaiting my confession?"

"Do you have something to confess?"

"If you believe that being gay is a sin, then perhaps. But having a twisted sexuality is worse."

"What do you mean by 'twisted'?"

"Those that can't decide which route to take to their desired destination. As for me, I've travelled only one road. That's what screwed Marlon up; not deciding is the worst choice of all." He pulled a lavender handkerchief out of his top pocket, dabbing his face and neck as though he were using a powder puff.

"Is that your view or his?"

"I don't know what he thought, but I could see his chagrin after we'd slept together. He didn't look like a man in love."

"In love? Where you were in love with him?"

Clive's ruddy cheeks betrayed his ultimate emotions.

"So the feelings weren't mutual then?" Theo could not stop himself.

"Marlon came from a very traditional family and was a player where women were concerned. You saw how Zoe was with him. He didn't want to throw that side of him away."

"Was being with you his first mistake?"

"My dear fellow, it is never a mistake to be with me."

Theo allowed a wry smile to grace his mouth, as he lapped up Clive's words and stored them for future use. "So you weren't his first?"

"I have to say, I feel as though you're interrogating me."

"Nonsense, I'm merely interested in your fascinating lifestyle."

Clive puffed out his chest for the first time in days. Theo believed he was going to garner enough information to use for several columns, when they were interrupted by Maggie returning with a pot of steaming coffee. The men accepted a top-up which gave her the chance to ask Theo a question. "I was wondering whether you and Alice had decided whether to stay on?"

"We have indeed," he replied, flashing a smile.

"We'll be delighted to have your company."

"And money, no doubt," chipped in Clive.

Maggie proffered a winsome smile, trying to maintain a cool and unruffled appearance. She hurried back to the kitchen to inform Marcus of the news.

"What was that comment for?" queried Theo.

"I overheard them discussing money worries and that they have no more bookings this month. You and Alice will have the place to yourselves, you lucky dogs."

"You seem more cheered than earlier, perhaps talking has helped you. I'll leave you to finish your coffee in peace."

Theo whisked himself away to write his column in peace. His fingers itched to be dancing over the keyboard.

No Fool Like an Old Fool

I said I'd soon have more to tell, and I do. Colin is a classic old fool in the sense that he fell in love with Mark. He actually fell in love. So he found himself in that unenviable position of stalking the very focus of his infatuation. Imagine the scene when Mark discovered Colin had booked a place on the same retreat. Imagine Mark's discomfort and Colin's exhilaration at sleeping in close proximity of one another. Had their clandestine meetings been more than mere conversation? I had the room between them and I wasn't aware of any shenanigans, which is sadly dull. Colin is chagrined about the possibility of his involvement with Mark's death, and if I were him and religious, I'd be hollering Hail Marys until I was devoid of breath.

I've many unanswered questions left, many of which sadly require Mark's input. One has to concur that Mark was a reluctant bi-sexual, and Colin had preyed on the vulnerable side of the man. Colin makes my relationship history look like a chapter in a Mills and Boon novel, and for that I'm most grateful. Or am I?

Theo smiled as he sent his work to Charles, before reaching over for his over-half-empty bottle of whiskey. One more day of everyone and then he would be alone with Alice. He hoped she would relax more and open up about her past.

Chapter 17

There was a strange mixture of mourning, melancholy, and euphoria amongst the guests on their last day. Clive was in the latter mood, knowing he was soon to be free of Marlon's ghost. Zoe, however, was draped in misery at the prospect of going home.

"I *so* wish I could stay a few days longer," she sighed.

"You'd be in the way with Theo and Alice. I think she'll be happier when we're not an audience to her carnal sojourn," replied Clive, savouring the last croissant he would eat in its native land.

"Do you think they'll still see each other back home?"

"It's feasible as they both live in London, but I doubt Theo will wish to carry it on."

"Why do you say that?"

Clive looked around the empty room before reducing his voice to a theatrical whisper. "He seems like an older version of Marlon to me."

"What, bi-sexual?"

"No, a player, a breaker of hearts."

"How could you possibly know that?"

"A man can sense it in another man. When we all first met, his eyes kept wandering all over you. He kept flitting around you like a fly trapped in a room, impatiently bashing into the window to reach the other side."

Zoe sat up straight, flicking her hair over her shoulder. "So why did he let me get cosy with Marlon?"

"Because he could see he was no match for a younger person, and he did not want to risk making a fool of himself." His eyes glistened.

Zoe sat back in her chair and sighed. "Well Alice has obviously got something I haven't."

"Her age," he grimaced, blotting around his mouth with a serviette.

An air of expectation arrived as Theo and Alice entered the dining room together. Maggie waltzed over to them and smiled. "The usual?"

"Seeing as this is your last day, let's all sit together?" suggested Theo, pulling out the chair next to Zoe.

Straightening her back, Zoe dipped her head and peered up at him from under her lush canopy of eyelashes. "We could spend the whole day together if you'd like."

Her coquettish look did not go unnoticed by Alice.

"Don't you want to use it to complete some writing?" she asked. "It's what you came here to do, after all."

"After Marlon's death, my muse evaporated. I could no more write than I could sheer a sheep."

Clive tugged at the neckline of his polo shirt. "I came to enjoy as much wine as possible. I pretended to write, much like you two?" He looked between Theo and Alice.

"I'm not the one pretending," announced Theo, admiring his own ability to bluff.

"And neither am I," added Alice. "This retreat has reignited my writing."

"I imagine that has more to do with Theo rather than the retreat itself," replied Clive, looking down his nose at her.

Alice blushed wildly. She was cross at Clive for being so impertinent, and even more irritated with Theo for not defending her.

"A writer must get inspiration from where they can," she whispered.

Theo enjoyed observing the social dances between his peers, storing pastiches for future columns.

"What about you, Theo? Do you wish to write now, or take a stroll with me to that bar in the village?" enquired Zoe.

Eager to garner more details about her, he took her up on the offer, deliberately avoiding Alice's glare. Her cheeks glowed as she rose from the table, asking Maggie if she could take her breakfast outside.

"Good idea, enjoy the clement weather whilst you can. I understand they're having quite wet weather back home."

"Nothing unusual there, then."

The fresh air cleansed her mind. The chateaux reeked of death since Marlon's departure, allowing thoughts of her mother to drift too deeply into her head. However, she wanted to stay longer for Theo; he wanted her to and she did not want to let him down. She wondered what her mother would say about her behaviour with him, and his behaviour with Zoe.

She jumped when Maggie placed her coffee and croissant in front of her. Holding the cup in her trembling hands, she focused on her surprisingly rapid emotional attachment to Theo, and wondered whether it was possible to fall in love at her age. Then a tinge of anger entered her mind at the thought of him with Zoe in their café.

The heavy stench of cigarette smoke gently wafted over her shoulder. She loathed that smell. Gauloises cigarettes were laced with an extra powerful blend of carcinogenic toxins that made her want to heave, and he was going to have to stop that habit once they returned home.

"So you're definitely writing today?" he asked, cocooned in a shroud of smoke.

"Of course. I still have a dream of becoming a published author. Don't you?"

Theo blew three smoke-rings. "I'm not sure what I want anymore."

Alice sensed a tinge of unhappiness in his voice and wanted to learn more, only to be interrupted by the arrival of Zoe.

"Ready for that stroll," she said, linking arms with him.

Theo stubbed his cigarette out underfoot and allowed himself to be led away. Alice watched the two figures recede into the distance towards the olive trees, and she found herself overwhelmed by a black hug of melancholy, restricting her ability to breathe.

"I've be wanting to come to this spot to exorcise Marlon's ghost before returning home, but I didn't want to come alone." She squeezed his arm, pulling herself in tighter to him, so her head nestled into his chest. "I'm so glad you're here with me. I feel safe."

Theo went to pat the side of her head, but stopped, realizing it was a fatherly gesture. His grip slackened.

"What's wrong?" she said, looking up to him.

"I suspect I look like a buffoon."

"It doesn't matter what others think, it's what you think about yourself that matters."

"Wise words from such a young head."

Zoe pulled him in the direction of the village, and he knew he was dabbling with the devil as he swaggered next to her.

Chapter 18

Clive and Zoe stood in the reception area with their suitcases at their feet whilst Maggie fussed around them and Marcus made up their bills.

"We'd love you both to visit us again," Maggie said as she hugged each of them. "I'm sure you'll have a more peaceful stay next time around."

Once Marcus had received payment he led the pair to the awaiting minibus and put their cases in the back. Zoe let her eyes linger on Theo before sliding into the seat.

As it disappeared into the dusk, everyone returned to the patio to enjoy the cooler air. Maggie brought out a chilled bottle of rosé and two glasses. "On the house, to wish you both a peaceful sojourn. And I'm glad you're taking the room with the double bed. We realise we should really buy more." She disappeared inside, leaving them alone.

"You're very quiet," said Theo.

"I was wondering how your day went with Zoe. You haven't mentioned it."

"And my silence conveys guilt, does it?"

"Avoiding the question doesn't help either."

"Fair comment," he said, pouring the wine. "She was certainly offering me an afternoon of pleasure, and I could easily have taken her up on the offer."

"That's reassuring."

"I said I could have, not that I did."

Alice traced the top of her glass with her finger, being careful not to give him eye contact. "So what did you do?"

"We visited the grizzly scene of Marlon's demise, then walked to the village to wet our livers."

"You went to our bar?"

"You knew that's where we were going, you could have come too. Besides, in case you hadn't noticed, there's a shortage of choice around here. I didn't take you to be the jealous type."

"I'm not," she interjected, "but I've made myself available to you and it's left me feeling rather vulnerable. Naturally, I'm a little uneasy about you spending time with a younger, more attractive woman."

Theo smiled before tipping the dregs of the glass into his mouth then pouring more. "What exactly are you hoping from our union?"

"I don't know exactly. I'm not sure what I'm supposed to expect."

"What happened to you?"

"I don't wish to talk about it; I'd rather just drink." She blushed, tilting her empty glass towards him.

"Secrets only sour the fruit of our souls, and inflict our face with crevices and scars of sacrifice and torture."

"That's flowery prose for a solicitor."

"I'm not defined by my job."

"Perhaps we could move inside?"

"Are you going to tell me about your past?"

"I just want a hug, is that okay?"

He shrugged, all the while wondering how he could extrapolate her secret.

Theo's snoring disturbed Alice. It was at moments like this she realized how old he was and in turn, how old she was becoming. Although part of her wanted to run screaming from the bed, another part of her wondered if he was her last chance of finding love and companionship.

Turning on her side, she propped herself up on her elbow to observe his rising and falling chest. Smatterings of grey hairs swirled around his nipples, in stark contrast to the darker ones; reminiscent of a badger. That thought made her smile.

After watching him for a few minutes, it dawned on her she had unintentionally given him her heart. But she could not help wondering how far things really went with Zoe, whose beauty and youth superseded her.

She quietly slid out from underneath the sheets and padded across the room to the window. The un-changing blue sky stretched across the horizon, hosting the occasional flock of birds or contrail from an aeroplane. Below her, Maggie was hanging out white sheets which billowed and gleamed in the sunlight. The scene looked idyllic, but it left Alice with a heavy heart, knowing that very soon she would be returning home to her noisy, empty flat.

Theo stirred behind her. "What's grabbed your attention out there?" he asked in a husky, morning voice.

"Just a tableau of peaceful country life," she replied, taking her dressing gown from the back of the chair.

Theo rubbed the top of his head vigorously and yawned before getting up. She watched his semi-naked form, in the reflection, walk towards the door to retrieve his sweatshirt.

"I feel rather like the consolation prize. The trophy you wanted has just returned to Britain." She paused. "Does that make me sound mad?"

"What's your problem now?"

"Are we going to continue this when we return home?"

He sighed. "You're moving too fast. Why don't we just enjoy what we have now?"

Alice pulled her dressing gown tightly around her before heading for the bathroom and slamming the door behind her.

She viewed her displeasing vision in the mirror before turning on the shower. As the water flowed, she wondered whether her insecurities would end up driving him away, causing a wave of nausea to buffer her.

Returning to the bedroom, she found Theo sitting at the desk, tapping away on his laptop. As she moved towards him, he lowered the screen and turned towards her.

"Feeling better?"

"I'm sorry about what I said. Can we just forget it?"

"Already done," he smiled. "I'm in the mood to write, so could you go down for breakfast and we'll meet up later?"

"You're so secretive about your writing; can't I take a peek?"

"Just get dressed and go, I can only write in peace."

Maggie was brushing the hallway, her clanking bangles jiggling up and down with each stroke.

"Shall I help myself to coffee if you're busy?" Alice asked.

"Gracious no, you're a paying guest, I'll get you breakfast. The temperature on the patio is very pleasant if you care to sit there. No Theo?"

"He's writing."

Alice entered the dining room expecting to see the absent guests sitting around the tables. Marlon appeared most frequently to her, as though his spirit haunted the chateaux, trapped by his *malheure*.

"Here you are," said Maggie, placing the coffee and croissant on the table.

"Have you got more guests coming?"

"When you two leave tomorrow, we have a couple and a single person coming. It's better than nothing but not the solid bookings we were hoping for."

"I'm sure it'll pick up, it's such a beautiful and peaceful place. I can't believe I'm leaving tomorrow. It's been dream-like here, on the whole."

"Forgive me for being nosy, but are you and Theo a confirmed couple?" Maggie interlocked her fingers behind her back.

"I'm not entirely sure."

Sensing Alice's embarrassment, Maggie blushed and withdrew to the kitchen, leaving Alice to enjoy the tranquillity of the early heat.

Theo had offered Alice new experiences and emotions which she could use in her writing, and for that she was eternally grateful. But he also left her feeling insecure and almost sullied; undesirable emotions to once again carry around with her.

Scratch Beneath the Surface of a Shy Shag

Anna has alluded to some troubling event in her past, but thus far has remained tight-lipped on the subject. But never fear, I still have tonight to pry it out of her. My guess is that perhaps she suffered some form of abuse, which has resulted in her stilted and frosty sexual performance between the sheets. Even her kissing lacks passion and warmth; there's no wonder she's single.

I'm taking my journalistic role too far, I hear you cry, but what better way to unearth the sleazy undercurrents in a writing retreat. After this, if your husband or wife says they're going on one, you know what to expect, and I'd advise you consider changing the locks whilst they're away.

Anna is following the classic neurotic female pattern of being jealous and possessive—neither are endearing qualities. She is also wanting me to heal her insecurities by confirming we'll continue this affair back in Britain. What do you think I'll do, readers?

He smiled at his deceitful and calculating behaviour; they were, after all, his best attributes.

Alice sat in the airy lounge writing notes for the denouement of her novel. She liked reading happy-ever-after novels, and so it was only fitting she wrote such an ending to her own.

The subplots needed to be tied off neatly, and a feeling of euphoria and wellbeing was required for the reader. As she jotted down her ideas, the feelings of elation told her she had got it right.

A refreshing breeze wafted in through the open doors, raising the muslin curtains like the spiritual dresses of angels. Through the gap in the curtains, Alice spied Theo talking to Marcus, who had become a rare sight since Marlon's death.

She stood up and walked to the window so she could watch him more closely, drink in his physical demeanour and commanding presence. *Oh God*, she thought to herself, *I* am *in love.*

Chapter 19

For their last evening together in the chateaux, Alice and Theo decided to have their meal, followed by a stroll to the bar in the village. Alice was saddened by her new emotions towards the bar since his trip with Zoe.

Since her time in France, her skin had become a gentle shade of toasted almond, and her demeanour had lightened. Melancholy thoughts of her mother were subsiding, gently being replaced by happier sentiments. But powerful fingers of her past still gripped her self-confidence, and she suddenly felt a desperate need to pry them off her.

She scrutinised herself in the mirror and decided the white t-shirt enhanced her hue. She spritzed on perfume and added a slick of lipstick as she waited for Theo to return from the bathroom, where he was getting ready.

When he returned, he was dressed in a beige linen shirt, creased from his second wear, and matching trousers. His skin had deepened in colour, and the broad flashes of white hair highlighted the waves.

"Ready?"

"Absolutely," she replied, locking the door behind her. She linked her arm through his, pulling him closer whilst their steps mirrored one another.

The dining room was filled with vases of fresh flowers, provided by Theo. The floral perfume floated on the gentle breeze coming through the open doors.

Theo pulled out the chair for her to sit down before taking his place opposite. Maggie brought over the bottle of chilled champagne, another gesture provided by Theo.

"Here's to a wonderful evening," he said as they clinked glasses. He watched her closely over the rim of his glass, trying to gauge where she was emotionally. "I want to get to know you better."

"Really?" her eyes widened. "I don't believe I have much more to tell you, or show you." She blushed wildly.

"We both have issues from our pasts and I feel we should exorcise the demons that haunt us. I've already mentioned mine."

"Your son."

"My relationship with him haunts me regularly."

"How exactly?"

"I have no one else to blame for the fact that I recoiled from my family due to my own selfish needs. I acknowledge my defects, but believe I have to stop looking at the past as it's dragging me down. Do you feel the same about your past?"

Alice took a few more sips of champagne to moisten her mouth. "My demons have been made bigger in my head over the years, and may in fact sound quite benign to you."

"Try me," he encouraged, topping up her glass.

"Thomas was my first boyfriend when I was nineteen," she began, "and I was totally in love with him." She stopped as Maggie arrived to see if they were ready to eat.

Theo waved Maggie away, then persuaded Alice to continue.

"I was a virgin and wanted to share my love with him in a special way, you know?"

He nodded, sitting upright with his hands in a prayer-like position on the table.

"I was just too naïve." Her eyes began to well-up. "He was this really handsome and popular guy at university, and I couldn't believe he'd even noticed me, never mind fancied me. I was nervous about him seeing me naked but he showered me with compliments about my body so I thought I had nothing to fear." She paused to sip her drink whilst Maggie put a baked Camembert in front of her.

"Did he treat you badly," whispered Theo, his forehead furrowed.

"Not in the way you think, he wasn't violent towards me." She paused to prod the melted cheese with a stick of celery. "We'd both had a fair amount to drink; Dutch courage for me, if you like."

Theo nodded.

"He persuaded me to undress in the light, draping a red silk scarf over a bedside light; I was hoping for complete darkness. I thought I heard him say something, but he said he'd just coughed." A slow, fat tear dribbled down her cheek.

Theo finished off his starter but Alice had hardly touched hers.

"So what happened?"

Alice sniffed. "*It* happened, but worse was to come." She waited for Maggie to take away their plates and replace them with their main course of chicken skewers and couscous. "He didn't want me to stay the night, which was disappointing. He didn't contact me for days after, and when I finally got hold of him he told me it was over as my body was repulsive and the sex was lamentable."

"Is that it?" he said incredulously.

"That was bad enough for a nineteen-year-old, but that's not what shattered my self-esteem. A week later, people around the campus began sniggering and whispering when they saw me; I'd become ostracized, and I couldn't understand why." She pushed her plate away, her meal untouched.

Theo listened intently. The champagne bottle was now empty, so he ordered a bottle of white wine and topped up both glasses.

"One day, a girl I'd never spoken to before came up to me in the library and told me she had seen a video of me going around. It was of me undressing and having sex with Thomas. Apparently, he'd done a piece to camera when I'd left the room, saying he'd won his bet, and he was desperate for a shower as it was the worst sex ever, and he needed to get the stench of me off him."

Theo stifled a guffaw, picking up his wine glass to hide his mouth behind. He ran through his next column in his head, eager to get it written.

"We do foolish things when we're young, and young men are the worst culprits."

"Are you defending him?"

"Not at all, but you shouldn't let that incident define you; you're a grown woman now."

She inhaled deeply. "I'm really sorry, but I don't fancy going to the bar now. Are you disappointed?" she whispered.

"Of course not. I'll stay down here to finish my meal, so you can go to sleep if you wish."

She gave a half-smile and left the table before Maggie returned to see she had not touched her meal.

The evening had turned flat, but Theo had what he wanted. He only had to pretend for a few hours more.

A few hours later after a lacklustre attempt at passion, Theo managed to crawl out of bed without disturbing her.

He moved silently to his desk and opened up his laptop.

Sex Tape

At last I can divulge what Anna's secret is. Brace yourselves, readers. When she was nineteen, she fell in love with a popular boy whom she briefly dated—we shall call him Tim. She should have asked herself why a handsome and popular boy would choose to date her, when clearly the university would have been inundated with more attractive and vivacious specimens. I think having fallen in love with him, she was truly blinded from the truth. She was a virgin, and he clearly wasn't—why would he be? She was drunk to dull her inhibitions, and he must have needed alcohol just to get into bed with her. We move forward to days after they'd slept together. Anna noticed people looking at her strangely and it was only when a library geek approached her, did she learn of the source of the pitying and mocking stares. Tim had recorded the event and passed the video around his friends until almost the whole campus had seen it. To add insult to injury, he had recorded a message at the end of the show stating that he'd won his bet and that she was a crap shag. Oh readers, she was still mortified when she recounted the story, and I had a job not to laugh in her face. She then concluded she suffered a mental breakdown, and left university without finishing her degree.

I have to say that Tim's analysis of her prowess in bed wasn't wrong. I thought she may have improved over the years, but she informed me she'd remained single ever since that time, so in fact, I was only the second man she'd ever slept with. She's hoping for us to continue our union back home, and why not, I'm devilishly handsome, but quite frankly, I've had more passion with a plate of profiteroles.

So there you have it, readers, a writers' retreat that has encompassed incompetent writing, suicide, and desperation of the carnal variety. If this is what aspiring authors do, then no wonder agents' slush piles are full of decidedly appalling crud which is only good for throwing into a wood burning stove.

I travel home tomorrow, for which I am eternally grateful.

He sent the column before closing the laptop and slipping it into the travel case ready for departure mid-morning. He turned to see Alice still enveloped in the quilt, blissfully unaware of his true feelings. He wished he had the ability to feel a modicum of remorse.

Chapter 20

Maggie was genuinely sad to see the pair leave.

"I do hope you'll both come back and stay, it's been such a pleasure having you here," she gushed.

Marcus stood by her side, giving Theo a flimsy handshake.

"I do hope we'll return in the near future," Alice whispered in Maggie's ear, her cheeks glowing brightly.

They both sat in silence in the minibus, taking the now familiar route through the village. As they passed the bar, Alice gave a rueful smile at the people sitting outside drinking coffee.

"I'll miss the sunshine and clear blue sky," he said as he looked through the window.

After a pause she spoke. "We haven't exchanged phone numbers. We should do that lest we forget in the madness of the airport." She rummaged around in her bag and found her notebook. She wrote her number and address down and tore out the page. "You can write your details in here," she said as she passed him the notebook.

Theo scribbled down his details and passed it back to her. She frowned at the scrawl.

"It's serendipitous we live close to one another. I often go to the Roman Road market and Victoria Park for concerts and festivals. We could occasionally go together."

"Perfect," he muttered, as he rubbed the tips of his four fingers along his forehead, attempting to erase the rumble of an approaching headache.

"I don't want to sound too pushy, but I wonder if you could tell me when we'll next meet?" she said cautiously.

"We haven't even left France yet. We'll meet up soon enough, don't fret. I'll call you."

Alice held her bottom lip between her teeth as she moved her hand close to his, slipping her fingers around his hand. She felt the hairs on the back of his hand against her palm; a sensation to treasure.

The airport bristled with people milling around the duty free area. Theo and Alice managed to find a couple of seats near the gate. She placed her handbag on her lap and squashed it against her stomach, trying to regulate her rapid heartbeat.

"When are you returning to work?" she ventured.

Theo did not react for a few seconds. "I'm sorry, I have a demon of a headache; even talking hurts my head."

Two hours later, they were settled into their seats on the plane. Alice was disappointed they were not sitting together, but when she turned around, his eyes were firmly shut, with vertical grooves slicing the flesh between his eyebrows.

The taxi drew up outside Alice's block of flats. She paid the driver before grabbing her case and rushing to the front door to avoid getting too wet in the pounding rain.

On opening the foyer door, she saw her post box crammed with junk mail hanging out of the flap, and a pile of newspapers on the top, which she had forgotten to cancel. Cursing herself, she scooped them up and gathered her post.

Once inside, she threw the papers on the dining table and dumped the case on her bed. The rumble of traffic in the background made her yearn for the sound of the cicada.

Pulling out her mobile, she checked for messages before throwing it on the table in disappointment. Switching on the kettle she picked up her post and flicked through it to find nothing of interest.

Wandering into the lounge she was reminded of how tiny her space was compared to the chateaux, and how soulless it was. The wallpaper and carpet were tired, not vintage, but just worn out from the years of depression that loomed within—not that she had recognised that at the time. It was as though she was seeing the place for the first time, pitying the inhabitants who must have lived a miserable existence there. But that was not true. She had fond memories of her mother, especially before her illness, and even after, there were still days of contentment.

She wanted to stop revisiting those memories, so she replaced them with thoughts of Theo. Images and memories of his scent cascaded into her mind, and she wondered whether he was thinking of her.

Theo pulled out a full packet of Gauloises from his bag and set them on the arm of his green leather chair. He poured himself a whiskey and after a few restorative sips, picked up the phone and dialled Charles's number.

"Well, how were my columns received?" he asked before lighting a cigarette.

"Bloody marvellous, the feedback is people are disappointed your time there is over. Are you smoking?"

Theo stopped blowing the smoke from his mouth and allowed it to trickle out instead. "Just a hangover from my time in France. I'm not returning to the habit."

"I hope not."

"So what happens now? Do I just return to reviewing books or have you got something else in mind?"

"Obviously your book work will continue, but how about doing an article reflecting on your time in France, and what, if anything, do you think writers gain from such an experience? If you can include Anna, then even better. Perhaps you'll see her in London, you old dog."

"Not bloody likely, but I'm sure I could make it an interesting read."

He punched the air on replacing the receiver. Life was looking up except for the headaches. He threw a couple of paracetamol into his mouth and washed them down with some tepid coffee he had to hand, before opening his laptop to make a start on a new article.

His thoughts drifted in the direction of Alice. He wondered how she had settled back into her solitary life, a life that by all accounts she was not in a rush to return to.

He massaged his temples as the dull pain in his head was not tempered by the pain relief tablets. The words on the laptop screen blurred, irritating him. He suspected he required reading glasses, but was too vain to visit an optician.

An hour later, the dull throbbing had subsided and his vision had regained clarity, so he set to work on his article.

Am I a Writer Yet?

If I were an aspiring author, I wonder what I would have gained from my week in France. Would I have come home fired up to finish my dream novel, or would I—as I suspect—come home feeling underwhelmed by the experience with maybe a sexually transmitted infection if I hadn't been careful?

Perhaps this isn't a fair commentary, seeing as the suicide dismantled the week. But let's focus on the days prior to that, and the guests who attended.

We had Dana and Elsie, the two older women who were frankly more suited to a crochet class than somewhere where the structure of writing would be analysed. Then we had Zara, who was writing an erotic novel, and who lived as though she were a character in her story. She threw herself at any man who looked at her, such was her desperation to be adored. She would make an interesting subject on her own, had I had more time with her.

Then there was Colin, who enjoyed the finer things in life, like powder-blue handkerchiefs, and young, muscular men. As it turned out, he wasn't even an aspiring author, just a stalker lusting after a man who regretted their sexual union. And this man was Mark, who was actually trying to write, but for whom his sexuality caused him pain like I've never witnessed before. Mark was doomed from the moment he sat on the plane, and I doubt that a posthumous novel will spring forth in the months to come.

So now we come to Anna. The winsome woman who works part-time in a bakery, and who aspires to be a writer of romantic fiction. A woman we come to learn has only had sex once in her life—before yours truly—and whose self-esteem has been whittled away over the years by the degrading and infantile actions of a university student.

She is neither charismatic nor stunning. She wears the badge of a repressed woman proudly on her lapel, as though that would attract the protector in a man. What she doesn't realize, the badge is a repellent, and I only overlooked it because I knew there'd be a story in her.

I was glad we only had a short time together as she was becoming very needy towards the end, and was pressing me to arrange a date back home. Being with her served a purpose in France, but I have no need or desire to meet up with her again. I could, and will, do so much better.

So, why did the owners decide to offer such a package when neither of them were writers? I posed this question and here is what they said. They believed they could offer writers a peaceful environment to work in, where they were provided with food and drink and plenty of space for people to write. They thought, mistakenly, that the writers would organize themselves into critique groups. I'm not sure they attained all they set out to do, but perhaps Mark's demise was to blame for that.

So would I recommend such a venue for wannabe writers? Well, firstly, I'd recommend you stay at a venue run by writers who would understand the needs of authors. And secondly, make sure your relationship back home is strong, lest you stray into someone else's bed for the week, and failing that, take plenty of condoms.

Theo sat back and rolled his shoulders, smiling to himself.

Meanwhile, Alice was gathering up the newspapers, when a contributor's name and picture on the front page caught her eye.

Chapter 21

Grabbing the newspaper, Alice looked more closely at the photo of Theo, or Theodore, as it was written on the banner of the front page. Her palms turned clammy as they gripped the paper.

Moving to the sofa, she flopped down with the paper resting on her lap. Her gaze flickered over his column as she slowly began to digest the enormity of what she was reading. Although he had used pseudonyms, it was quite clear to her who was who. He was demeaning and derisive of the whole group, and dreadfully mocking of her and her attempts at flirting with him. She threw the paper to the floor and dashed to the bathroom. Acrid tears cascaded down her nostrils as the heaving continued to empty her stomach, culminating in her collapsing on the floor in a crumpled heap.

She remained there trying to compose herself. The bathroom walls were closing in, and the floor undulated beneath her, as the rapid breathing of a panic attack began crushing what strength she had left. *Did he write about our lovemaking*, she wondered, pulling herself up using the side of the bath. She had to read on.

Staggering to the lounge, she perched gingerly on the sofa, retrieving the rest of the papers and scattering them at her feet. She picked them up one by one and put them in date order, aware that another article could be in the offing as they had only just returned home.

Rain pelted against the window, mirroring the tears lashing down her face as she read each column.

He depicted her cruelly in a way she had never perceived herself. He talked about her insipid presence and image, and even mentioned he suspected a secret in her past; a secret he vowed to uncover.

She threw the paper to one side, scrabbling around for the next one.

She fell upon the column titled "Scratch Beneath the Surface of a Shy Shag." Mortified, she read on, gasping and sobbing at his description of her dimpled dough-like thighs, her ineffectual movements in bed, and her lips which were reminiscent of sundried tomatoes.

The tears stopped suddenly, replaced by bubbles of anger which burst into the air like mini mortar shells. Her body shook and she felt numb, no longer knowing how to feel or think.

She traipsed around her flat, sapped of energy but with her mind raging, as she tried to work out what to do, when she suddenly remembered she had his contact details. Snatching her bag from the table she tipped it upside down and found her notebook.

She picked up the phone and dialled.

"Of course, it's the wrong number," she screamed to the wall.

Not since the day of her mother's death had she felt so low. She hated herself for being so weak and pathetic, and she thanked God her mother was not alive to witness her situation.

Thoughts of contacting the newspaper spun around her head, but she imagined he would refuse to take her call, telling the staff she was the deranged stalker from the retreat who should be shunned at all cost. A wry smile crossed her lips as she thought how she had been right all those years; men were not to be trusted, especially when one is a plain-looking woman.

Her appetite vanished, and her heart shrivelled to an empty husk. Shuffling to bed, she cared not that it was only mid-afternoon, the day had nothing left to offer her.

Theo was taken by surprise by a sudden pang of loneliness in the early evening. It was then he realised it would be the time of day he and the other guests would meet for an aperitif on the patio. He would listen to them prattle on about their literary prowess or writer's block, mocking them silently in his head.

His thoughts drifted to Alice, and how unlike she was to his soon-to-be remarried ex-wife, Joanna, who was demanding, dismissive, aloof, and argumentative. Joanna could crush the life out of any man who crossed her path.

But Alice was different. She made him feel appreciated, funny, and clever; she probably knew she was punching above her weight. But whatever the reason, Alice was more companionable than Joanna had ever been. Had he thrown something away just because the packaging was not fancy enough?

He poured a whiskey, when suddenly he was overcome by a wave of nausea; the whiff of alcohol turned his stomach. He put the glass to one side and retired to his leather armchair to let the sensation pass.

The following morning, Theo felt refreshed. He had swept aside his thoughts of Alice, putting his doubts down to feeling unwell and sorry for himself.

Charles had called first thing, requesting a meeting regarding future projects, and as he hankered company, it suited him.

He finished his coffee and toast and packed his bag for his excursion, but without warning, another wave of nausea knocked him sideways, making him dash to the bathroom. The air was quickly sullied with a fetid smell that no amount of air freshener would dispel.

Much as he wanted to see Charles, he felt it was too risky to travel on the tube whilst his stomach was feeling so dodgy. And as much as he detested visiting his doctor, he decided it was time to break the habit.

Alice had been awake for hours, cutting Theo's columns from the papers, re-reading them, and drinking copious amounts of coffee.

The weather outside was grey and overcast, in dour contrast to the resplendent French weather. With a leaden heart, she shoved her arms into her coat sleeves and headed off to work.

Pulling her hood over her head, she traced the cracks in the pavement as she walked towards the bus stop, feeling a heavy weight crush her shoulders and neck. As she mooched along the route, someone bumped into her shoulder, almost knocking her over, and failed to apologize for their action. That insignificant encounter was enough for her to burst into tears. She turned, almost running, and headed back home, where she threw herself onto her mother's bed and sobbed deeply into the pillow.

"I haven't seen you for a long while," said Doctor Stone as Theo walked into her office.

"I only visit you when I can't cure myself," he smiled, settling down on the hard wooden chair, resting his hands in his lap. "I've been suffering with bouts of nausea and vomiting, and no, it's not my cooking."

Doctor Stone proffered a gentle smile. "I know you would only come in if you were truly debilitated by it. Have you also had any headaches or visual disturbances?"

Theo recounted his blurred vision and dull headaches then answered her questions, saying he was not stressed, and he did not drink too much. He omitted his recent brush with French wine and cigarettes.

She gave him a physical before raising an eyebrow. "I'd like to send you for an MRI, just to be safe."

"Safe about what?"

"I'm not exactly sure, but humour me, Mr Edwards."

He walked out of her office dismayed at not having a quick solution, like a bottle of pills. Worry wriggled into his mind on the tube journey, but by the time he got home he had replaced his anxiety with thoughts of Alice.

Alice took her sick note from the doctor and walked slowly out of the surgery. Their conversation was a blur with only the odd word sinking into her mind. The main word being *depression*.

The doctor believed it was a culmination of her mother's death, her recent brush with Theo, and loneliness. Alice owned up to it as though she were in a confessional booth. As well as a sick note and a prescription, the doctor suggested she investigate some form of evening class or volunteering to engage in. All that seemed impossible in her current state, but the doctor said the tablets would work in a couple of weeks, then hopefully she would have the drive to move forward.

Counselling was also offered, and all she had to do was phone the number on the leaflet to arrange an appointment. Scrunching it up, she shoved it in her pocket.

The foyer door felt heavier than usual. Her post box was empty, then she noticed the newspaper on the top, and wondered whether it was safe to read.

On opening her front door, the tenacity of her mother's lavender scent in the flat had finally been replaced by the scent of lemons, thanks to the candles dotted around the rooms, although Alice still smelt lavender periodically.

Putting her sick note in an envelope to post, she was awash with relief at not having to blend in with society for the time being.

Chapter 22

Theo was surprised to hear Joanna's voice on the phone. She launched into a rant about Justin's current situation, and did not pause for breath until her final damning phrase: "I blame you for this."

"It's hardly my fault if our son's fallen in with the wrong crowd. He's twenty-one for God's sake."

"He was doing well educationally until you decided to attend a strip club and go a little too far with a young tart," she spat.

"How many times do I have to apologize for my midlife crisis?"

"You'll never be forgiven."

"What a surprise," he muttered under his breath. "Anyway, you surely didn't phone just to lambast me, what do you want?"

"Much as it pains me, we need to meet with Justin and see how we can straighten him out. His drug use has got out of control, and he's got his finals coming up. His tutor says he's not even completed his project."

"It's a bit late to tell us now."

"You just can't be bothered to help, can you? You always were a useless man and father."

"I didn't say I wouldn't help, I just said it's perhaps a little late for his exams. But I do want to help him."

"Right then, I'd rather meet somewhere neutral but as I don't want to air our dirty linen in public, you'll have to come here."

He sensed she was hurting underneath her anger. "When?"

"I'm collecting him this afternoon, so tomorrow morning at ten. Goodbye."

He was left listening to the dialling tone before replacing the receiver, but the sharpness of her voice and words continued echoing around his head.

He had not seen his son for four years and now they were to meet over the contentious issue of drugs. The meeting was taking place in the near-million-pound marital home he had handed over to Joanna without compunction. He still missed it terribly.

He made a coffee and wandered out into his overgrown garden. The sun was trying to pierce through the clouds and the leaf laden branches, in the hope of spreading dappled light on the mossy stone path. Woody lavenders, badly in need of a prune, displayed deep purple tips, and the boarder housed an anomalous array of perennial plants, shrubs, skeletons of leaves left over from autumn, and a twisted array of weeds.

Walking to the end of the garden, he brushed dried whitish-grey bird droppings from the wooden bench and sat down. Cupping the mug in both hands, he inhaled the aroma of strong coffee, letting it seep into every crevice of his mind.

The machinegun sound of a magpie's call broke his reverie, rocking him back to thoughts of his son. How had straight-laced Julian got in with the wrong crowd, let alone into the denigrating world of drugs?

He had been a rather typical teenager in that he had no respect for his parents or his home. His attitude towards them left them reeling in his wake. However, he did not smoke, drink excessively, steal, or sleep around, as far as they were aware. All that may have changed over the years, but he remembered Justin saying that people who smoked or took drugs were "moronic," and he had no time for them; he had even lost friends who indulged whilst still at school.

And now he was to believe his son was wasting his university degree due to becoming one of those moronic idiots he once despised.

As if sensing his troubles, Rufus padded towards him and leapt onto his lap. He really should take that bottle of wine round to Joyce to thank her for cat-sitting, he thought to himself.

He decided to turn his attention to the article Charles had requested. He moved back inside and sat at his desk, before opening his laptop and staring at the blank screen—a writer's nemesis. He trawled his memories for ideas pertaining to the requested topic, and within a few minutes, his mind flooded the screen.

Post Retreat Blues

The further away in time I get from being at the retreat, the more I find I'm actually missing being around the other guests. I sense you thinking I've turned soft, but read on.

I'm actually missing observing the group, not being in their company. The person I miss the most, strangely enough, is Anna, as she made me feel good about myself in the light of her being such a failure. She gave up any chance of a life to care for her sick mother, or at least that's what she'd have us believe. My view on people who do that is they don't have a scintillating career or an interesting life in the first place. They probably have below average intelligence, are possibly friendless, and only have mundane jobs, if they work at all. Caring for a sick relative is just the excuse they needed to opt out of society and the work merry-go-round.

Now you may feel that's a harsh judgment on a section of the community, but I'm not known for my niceties. I know you don't disapprove of my writing, as my columns have been well received, so I imagine very little of what I write here will actually rile you.

I do have Anna's mobile number, but I gave her my false details in return, as what would she have to give me now? We're no longer in the warmer climes of France, where the flowing wine and Gauloises put a man in the mood for something normally too ordinary for his palette.

Of course, I didn't tell her, or any of the group, about my true profession, otherwise they wouldn't have trusted me. You have my gift of deception to thank for these delectable columns.

I wonder what the others are doing now that they're back. Colin will undoubtedly be trawling the gay bars and clubs; the two older women will still be knitting and making up wild, wishful tales, and recounting with horror the day they found a man hanging in a tree; Zara will be flirting with every man she sees to fulfil her need to be the centre of attention, whilst dining-out on dating a man who committed suicide; and Anna will be wondering how to fill her empty vessel of a life now that her mother is dead, and her dreams of being a novelist are too lofty for her talent. They were des-

perately sad beings to start with, and they remain the same, with the added layer of still being unfulfilled writers on their return home.

He rubbed the back of his neck as he felt another headache rumbling in the background. Maybe he should sit up straighter, or visit the optician as his doctor suggested along with the MRI. But for now, he was going to contemplate tomorrow's daunting meeting with a whiskey and one of the few remaining Gauloises.

Theo woke up dreading the meeting with the family he had so publically deserted. That was how the situation was viewed, even though it was Joanna who had thrown him out, and it was Justin's choice not to see him.

Justin, the son he could not comprehend. On the one hand, he felt a pang of guilt, but on the other hand, at seventeen he was old enough to deal with his parents' separation. Perhaps Justin had hoped they would get back together seeing as they never actually divorced. Perhaps it was the finality of the divorce which triggered his drug abuse, or perhaps he just did not like his mother's new beau. Why did it always have to be his fault?

He felt like he was walking through treacle as he trudged towards the underground. The hairs on the back of his neck stood to attention the closer he got.

The air in the underground was grimy and sticky. Beads of sweat bubbled up on his face as he studied the film posters on the wall, none of which appealed to him.

A dusty breeze funnelled down the platform as a train approached, sticking particles of dirt to his clammy face. Everyone shuffled forward so when the doors opened it was difficult for people to get on and off, but after a few minutes of shoe scuffing, and shoulder barging, Theo managed to find a seat.

The morning sun blinded him as he re-emerged from the underground station. He felt at home in North London, and he loved living in Highgate for its relative peace whilst still being close to the city centre. He hesitated to admit it hurt more to leave the area than it did to leave his marriage.

Standing outside the black wrought-iron gates his heartbeat thudded in his temples. From the exterior, the house looked the same. It loomed over him with its pure white façade and Grecian pillars either side of the glossy black front door. The box hedge was manicured to perfection, and the York stone path was swept clean of any garden debris. The window boxes were burgeoning with colourful plants, and the sun bounced off the pristine window panes.

He lifted the trunk of the large brass elephant head and knocked.

"Late as per usual," Joanna said in a clipped tone on opening the door.

"Trouble on the tube," he lied.

The imposing marble fireplace in the lounge was filled with a gigantic vase of peace lilies, and silver-framed, black and white family photographs were aligned perfectly along the mantelpiece. None of him, of course.

Justin was slouched at one end the sofa staring at the large flat-screen TV. He made no acknowledgement of their entrance. Joanna grabbed the remote and switched it off, only for Justin to continue staring resolutely at the blank screen.

"We need to talk," Joanna stated, sitting at the other end of the sofa and crossing her legs. "Blanking us isn't going to make this go away, you know."

"And what will it actually achieve?" he replied in a deeper tone than Theo expected.

"Hopefully a First in your degree and a well-paid job after that," replied Joanna.

"Of course, money is the driving force in your life, Mum."

"What's your degree in," asked Theo.

"Oh that's right, *Dad*, you've no idea what your only child's studying, do you?"

"If you'd have wanted to keep in touch, I—" Theo stopped after getting a steely glare from Joanna.

"There's plenty of time to discuss your father's failings, but for now I want us to focus on *your* current situation."

Theo decided to continue taking an active role in the conversation. "What drugs are we talking about?"

Justin rolled his eyes, exhaling loudly. "Only weed, nothing more than what you two did in your youth."

"We smoked cannabis, but today, it's far more pure and potent stuff. There's a link to future mental health issues with skunk, you know?" Theo rebutted.

Joanna turned to him as he sat down in a bucket chair next to the window, raising her eyebrows as much as she could after the Botox injections. "How do you know that?"

"I'm a journalist, and I read a lot. If you read more substantial articles, you'd know too. How long have you been smoking it?" He turned his attention back to Justin.

"Years, but I can stop if I want to, I'm not addicted."

Theo laughed. "That's exactly what addicts say. Do you take anything else?"

Justin slumped further into the sofa so it looked like he was being eaten by a fabric monster.

"Your tutor told me you also drink a lot," Joanna added.

"For God's sake, you two think you're so omnipotent," he snapped, sweat glistening over his cheeks. "You've no right talking to me like this when you're incapable of being civil with one another. You're like bloody children. I'm like this 'cause of you, and I hate you both." And with that, he shot out of his seat and stormed out of the room, slamming the door firmly behind him.

"Well, that went well."

"Oh don't be so flippant, Theodore. I asked you here to help, not act like my second child."

"I can see the time apart hasn't softened you towards me," he quipped.

"Sorry, I know, we should focus on Justin. But blaming us after all this time, really?"

"Our separation obviously pained him more than we knew."

"He's young; he should be looking forward, not re-visiting his past to plaster his soul with pain."

"You do talk flowery rot at times. Is that what women fall for?"

"I thought we were here to sort out our son, not examine my love life."

"Touché."

They sat in a suffocating silence for a few minutes before Joanna suggested they go and find Justin. Theo eased himself out of his chair and followed her to the large, sunny kitchen. Through the French window they saw Justin sitting on a bench smoking, billowing clouds of dirty grey smoke entombing him.

"I hope that's not what I think it is," said Joanna as she tripped over the step into the garden.

Justin saw his parents marching towards him and stubbed his rollup under his biker boot. "Chill, it's only a cigarette. I roll my own, fewer chemicals that way," he said as he saw his mother's icy stare.

"Still carcinogenic. I'm so disappointed," she sighed.

"Your tutor said you got in with the wrong crowd, but I always thought you were stronger than that," said Theo.

"You know nothing about me. You don't even know whether I'm a leader or a follower."

"You're right, I don't know the young man you've turned into, but I do remember the little boy who once ran around this garden hunting Easter eggs, and the teenage boy who played damn awful music in his bedroom, so loudly the windows rattled. You're not a total stranger."

Justin shrugged, stretching out his long limbs and rocking the heels of his boots in the gravel. The scrunching noise grated on Joanna, who sighed loudly.

"Hell, Mum, everything has to be quiet and perfect to please you. I couldn't wait to go to uni to get away from you."

She narrowed her eyes as Theo noticed tears brimming behind the steely glare.

"Don't be so unkind to your mother, she's always loved you and built up a highly successful business whilst raising you."

Joanna turned to Theo, slack jawed and wide-eyed. "You never defended me when we were married, why now?"

"He wants you back now that you're going to marry another guy."

"Justin!" they cried in unison.

He skipped back towards the house laughing maniacally.

Chapter 23

Alice traipsed back up to her flat with the latest newspaper. It had been three days since she had been signed off work, during which time she had ensconced herself in her flat eating crisps and bowls of cereal. She had lost confidence in her writing, and even stopped participating on social media sites. In fact, she had withdrawn from life as much as possible, struggling with her mood that was becoming darker as time progressed.

She filled the kettle and sat down at the table to read the paper. Her heart stopped momentarily as she saw Theo's name on the front-page banner. She turned to the appropriate page to read his article entitled, "Am I a Writer Yet?" *Will he ever stop?*

When she was finished reading, globules of salty water dribbled down her cheeks, pooling in the corners of her mouth. Sobs burst forth like she was being given the Heimlich manoeuver as her tears spat out, smudging the inky paper.

She pressed the flat of her hand against her chest and moved to the window, looking down at the scene below. What would it be like to fall?

She staggered backwards and crumpled into the chair, brushing her hand along the table to send the sheets cascading to the floor. She hurt in places she never knew could hurt, and she so wanted a hug from her mother.

What would her mother suggest, she wondered. She closed her eyes tightly and listened to see if she could hear her voice, only to hear her doctor's voice instead. "Don't sit around prevaricating, start a hobby or do some volunteering."

Two hours later, wearing a knee-length denim dress and a shrug to hide her upper arms, she closed the door behind her and headed for the library.

She skulked in the shadows along the edge of the pavement and was relieved to step inside the imposing building, where the familiar peace was like a child's comfort blanket wrapped around her heart, keeping her safe from all the terrifying monsters.

Several people were sitting at the computers, whilst a group of mums and toddlers were sitting on the floor in a semi-circle being read to by one of the librarians. Alice passed the community notice board announcing future readings by local authors, church fetes, and school concerts. In the bottom right-hand corner was a notice from the local hospice asking for volunteers to read to the guests or just sit and talk to them. The doctor's words bounced around her head once more. Scrabbling around her handbag, she found her notebook and pen and jotted down the details.

Alice hurried into her flat with three novels, one poetry book, and a book on the meaning of flowers. As she closed the door behind her, her heart pounded in her chest, and droplets of sweat were dribbling down her spine.

Once the kettle was switched on, she turned her attention to the note about the hospice; a place she knew nothing about except that it was a place for people to die peacefully, and it only survived on charitable donations.

Taking a deep breath, she picked up the phone.

Theo sat in the stark white waiting room dressed in a green-and-white-checkered hospital gown, with his clothes and watch removed. On the table next to him sat a pile of dog-eared magazines and a folder containing the hospital protocol. Two other people, also in gowns, sat along with him, but nobody spoke or made eye contact.

"Mr Edwards, this way please," said a young woman in a white lab coat. Theo wondered whether all the white was supposed to equate to a closeness to heaven and angels.

He followed the woman into a room where a machine resembling a giant packet of Polos stood in the centre. She rechecked that he had nothing metal on him then asked him to lie on the panel that would move him into the cylinder.

It felt cold, hard, and unforgiving. The woman pulled a cage over his head before pushing polystyrene pieces between his head and the cage to wedge it in place, then handed him a button on a cord to press if he needed help. "Have you brought a CD to play?"

"I prefer the silence," he replied.

"I'm afraid you'll find it very noisy in there, but not to worry, it'll only take about twenty minutes."

Closing his eyes, he began moving into the machine at a snail-like pace. He tried focusing his mind on the book he was currently reading instead of the sensation of claustrophobia that was mounting in his brain. The clunking and humming noises were disconcerting, and he wished he had brought a CD along as had been suggested.

Twenty minutes later as he started moving out of the machine, he felt every pore on his body prickle with sweat, and his ears were ringing with the noise. Easing himself down the couple of steps, he returned to get dressed, before cautiously strolling outside to find a taxi.

Once home, he made his way to the kitchen and twisted the cap off the bottle of whiskey before pouring a large measure. After taking a Gauloises from the packet in the drawer, he stepped into the garden and sat on the bench. How good it felt to be outdoors, he thought to himself as he inhaled the noxious fumes.

Alice brushed flecks of dust from her skirt as she stood outside the elongated bungalow. Before she had the chance to ring the bell, a woman opened the front door and welcomed her in.

"Alice Calwin, I presume? I'm Sadie Horne. Welcome," she said, thrusting a hand towards Alice.

Sadie's grip was firm and her smile engaging, but Alice doubted her own likeability in front of such competence.

"I'll show you around and then we can have a chat in my office. Do you know much about a hospice?"

"Not really."

"People think we only offer palliative care to people with illnesses such as cancer, multiple sclerosis, motor neuron disease, Parkinson's, and end-stage dementia. Of course we do that, but not only that. Some people only stay for a few days to get their symptoms under control. We accept anyone regardless of religion, sexuality, or gender, and our service is free of charge. This is the day room," she said, opening the door to a bright room with buttercup-yellow walls, and floor-length windows overlooking a landscaped garden and a fish pond with a gently spouting water fountain in the centre.

People turned to face them; their faces not forlorn and twisted with pain and fear as Alice expected, but smiling and peaceful.

"We have an occupational therapist offering a range of activities," Sadie continued, waving her arm at people playing dominos and painting.

Alice managed to smile before Sadie whisked her into the garden.

"Gardening can be therapeutic. We have these raised beds so people in wheelchairs can still enjoy touching and smelling the flowers, as well as planting them. We have a scented border comprised of lavenders and buddleias, with plenty of benches and quiet areas for friends and families to sit with their loved one."

"I thought it would be depressing here, but it's not."

"That's good to hear. We aim for a happy, calm, positive, and comfortable environment for all involved."

They walked down a corridor where all eight ensuite bedrooms were situated. Soft music filtered out from one of the rooms.

After the tour, they returned to Sadie's office.

"What made you decide to volunteer here?" she asked.

"My doctor suggested I try volunteering," she blushed.

"That's not uncommon. Some people come here as they have a fear of death, some because they lost someone recently, some are lonely, and some because they want to do something positive with their free time."

"I tick all those boxes," Alice said, looking at her hands.

"That's not a problem. What we don't want is people foisting their religious views on our guests, or thinking they can cure people with prayers or magic."

Alice frowned, not sure if she needed to say anything. "I lost my mother recently and had no thoughts about healing her in any way. I just wanted her to be peaceful and comfortable in the time she had left."

"I'm sorry for your loss, Alice. What do you think you can offer us here?"

"I thought I could perhaps read to people if they wished."

"Many people do like that, especially if their vision is impaired. Some people want to chat or go for a stroll in the garden. I'm sure someone like you will fit in very nicely. We'll just wait for your police check to come through and then you can start. What days are good for you?"

Alice was stunned at being accepted there and then, and found herself offering any day as long as she had plenty of time to do her writing.

"What do you write?"

"Romance."

"Have you been published?"

Alice hated that question. "Nothing so far."

Sadie looked disappointed and Alice hated that too.

Alice trembled as she left St. Lydia's. She sensed her mother smiling down on her and her mood lifted slightly. "I'm going to be all right," she uttered as she ambled back to the bus stop.

Chapter 24

Theo sat in Doctor Stone's office waiting for her to finish reading the letter on her desk; her pensive look troubled him. She exhaled loudly through her nose as she sat back before looking straight at him.

"Something has shown up on your MRI. You'll be sent an appointment to see the consultant shortly."

"Clearly it's bad news."

"They can't be sure, but taking your symptoms into consideration, it's possible you may have a brain tumour. But it's not the end of the road, further investigations will tell us more, like what treatment can be offered."

"Meaning whether it's operable or not, I suppose."

"There are other treatments available, but we're jumping ahead of ourselves. Let's take this one step at a time and see what the consultant has to say. I know you're no great fan of visiting the surgery, but if you need to talk, my door's always open."

Theo gave her a lopsided smile before walking out, numb to the sounds of other people around him. *I could be dying*, he pondered to himself. *God.*

"I had a ferocious row with Justin last night after I caught him drinking Jack Daniels straight from the bottle. You've got to sort him out."

Theo held the phone away from his ear as Joanna's shrill voice screeched down the line. Pinching the bridge of his nose, he tried to think of what to say. His son was a stranger to him, his relationship with Joanna was exceedingly strained, and he did not know how long he had to live. But it was not the time for recrimination; he had to find a way to bring mother and son together. They may only have each other soon.

"I'll come round this afternoon and see what I can do," he offered.

"I need you to speak with him, not be your usual cocky, arrogant self. You're not exactly renowned for allowing others to have their say."

"What, like you I suppose?"

"Don't be so bloody condescending. I've had to deal with Justin through his terrible teens *alone*, whilst you gadded about."

"Do you want me to come over or not?" He did not mean to raise his voice; it just happened.

"Showing your true colours, eh?"

His knuckles blanched as his grip tightened on the receiver. "I'll be round at two," he said before disconnecting.

His head hurt with the stress. How was he going to get through to Justin without mentioning his own health; he did not want to emotionally blackmail him into forgiving him and loving Joanna. He hoped inspiration would come to him as he sipped coffee and stared at the mass of neglected foliage rambling freely in his garden.

There was nothing Alice could do after sending the forms to the police, but wait. She was uplifted by her interview, but as the days passed, she felt the black cloud of depression cast its shadow over her once more, as she sank further into the dank cavern she hovered near constantly.

She wandered into her bedroom and pulled out a shoe box from under her bed to retrieve Theo's paper clippings. The springs squeaked as she sat on the bed and opened the box.

She re-read every word he had written as a form of self-harm, and let each syllable carve blistering wounds on her heart. No matter how many times she tortured herself, a part of her still loved him, and that angered her. How was it possible to be betrayed by someone, yet still ache for their touch? Love had a lot to answer for.

She let her finger pass over the picture of Theo, believing he could sense her touch. The picture was small, but if she stared intently she could see the sharp intrigue in his eyes that made her feel special at the time. She replaced the cuttings in the box and closed the lid, blinking rapidly before shoving it under her bed and moving to the kitchen.

Her novel had become her only companion over time, and yet she was struggling to find the right words, in fact, any words. She wondered if her anti-depressants were affecting the sharpness of her mind, but even if they were, she needed them. Life had too many jagged edges for her to damage herself on.

The male protagonist in her novel had morphed into Theo, with his tall frame, large hands, and enquiring hazel eyes. She liked spending time with him each day, time where she was in control of the situation, and his behaviour.

She missed him. She missed drinking wine with him and smelling his citrus scent mixed with the stench of cigarette. She missed his touch, his smile, and being hugged by his hirsute arms, and she hoped writing about him would obliterate the pain that engulfed her every moment of every day.

Theo managed to arrive exactly at two o'clock at Joanna's house to find Justin sitting on the doorstep, smoking a rollup. He was wearing a scruffy designer t-shirt, and vintage denim cropped jeans with frayed edges.

"Waiting for me?" Theo asked.

"Not especially. Mum won't let me have a house key. I've just been to buy some baccy, and I get back to find she's gone out."

Theo noticed the absence of her Mercedes and wondered what she was playing at. Still, it gave him the opportunity to talk to Justin alone. He moved forward and sat down on the step next to him.

"Could you roll me one?"

Justin's eyes narrowed. "This isn't your idea of getting down with the kids is it?"

"Good God no. I rekindled the habit in France and I just fancied one. Anticipating a meeting with your mother brings it out in me."

"You haven't been together for years and yet you're still blaming her for your failings. You're pathetic."

"Well thanks for the vote of confidence, son. Now how about we have a frank discussion about your current situation, or are you going to blame me for that?"

Justin was engrossed in making a rollup, his head down so his floppy fringe hid most of his face. "I'm just not sure where I'm going with all of this. I don't fancy joining the rat-race and working my butt off to then hand over forty percent of my wages to the government in tax."

"You can't start worrying about those kind of things; they're not important right now. You must have some passion in life that inspires you."

Justin handed him the rollup then looked away. "I'm not like you. You've always had a passion for reading and the English language, and Mum loves designing and running her business."

Theo lit his rollup and inhaled. The harshness was reminiscent of a Gauloises, without the distinctive, pungent aroma.

"Do you only smoke these?"

"They're better with a bit of skunk in them. Fancy a joint?"

"That would truly aid the situation, Joanna turning up to find us both stoned on the doorstep."

"At least we'd be bonding."

Theo smiled and shook his head slowly. "I do want to get to know you better, but I also want you to be close to your mum again."

A car pulled up to the curb and Joanna got out, pushing her sunglasses on top of her head. She moved swiftly towards them, her heels clicking on the pavement.

"Thanks for being a tremendous role model," she snapped.

Theo, crushed his tab end underfoot before following the pair into the vast entrance hall, where Joanna dumped her bag and linen jacket. Justin strode to the kitchen and grabbed a can of Coke from the American fridge. His parents followed, only to stand around waiting for something to happen, until Joanna finally broke the silence.

"I want Justin to go back to university and finish his degree. After then we can look at the future."

"I don't want to go back. You can't make me," Justin spat.

"Tough, you can't come back here then, it won't work out."

Theo watched the two people he used to be close to tear strips off each other, hurling wounding words that would come back to haunt them in the future.

He leant against the door frame. "What's worrying you about going back? Is it the work or are you worried about bumping into the old crowd?"

"Neither, Einstein. The degree won't give me much, apart from starting at a very low position in the TV world. I'm just not rocking it anymore."

Puffing out her cheeks, Joanna clamped her hands on her bony hips. "I told you *that* when you chose that degree. Anyway, I always taught you to finish what you'd started."

"What, like you and Dad did with your marriage? Practise what you preach, Mother dear."

"Damn you. I won't tolerate your impudence anymore. Do something, Theodore."

A rush of nausea swooped over him as he grabbed the door frame to keep himself upright. His mouth puckered and tasted disgusting thanks to smoking. "Could I have a glass of water?" he asked no one in particular.

"Don't play the wounded man, Theodore. He's your son too. Why doesn't he go and live with you then, after his degree?"

"I *am* in the bloody room. I've told you what I want to do. Why is no one listening to me? I hate you both, and I hate stupid dick-face Rory."

"Well he's had it up to here with you," she replied, waving the flat of her hand just about her head. "He's become rather hesitant about marrying me because of you. I won't lose my future husband just to please my ungrateful son." Her pitch had become so high, Theo believed only dogs in the neighbourhood could hear her.

The water settled his stomach and cleansed his mouth, so he pulled out a chair for Joanna and then one for himself. They both sat opposite Justin who was now chewing the skin around his thumbnail.

"Do you really hate us, Justin?" Theo asked.

"I can't remember a time I loved *you*, and Mum and I are going through a rough patch. She can't admit I'm grown up and that I don't need to live by her rules anymore."

"You damn well do in my house," she exclaimed.

Theo felt the spike of Justin's words pierce his heart. In the past he would not have cared, but now he needed to go in peace, with those around him professing they will miss him, not jump for joy at his departure.

"I want him to finish his degree. At least then he'll have something to show for the three years he spent there," she continued.

"Do you have a job?" Theo asked.

"Yeah, in Tesco, why?"

"If you finish your degree, I'll match whatever you've saved so you can go travelling for a year."

Joanna flashed him a cold look, but Justin sat up in the chair, flicking his fringe out of his eyes with a jerk of his head. "Do you mean that?"

"Of course I do. Perhaps a gap year will help you sort your head out."

"Sort his head out? What the hell does that mean?"

"Get some direction in life is perhaps a better way of describing it," replied Theo, quickly raising an eyebrow to Justin, who was now fully engaged in the conversation.

"What if I fail my degree?"

"You can re-sit, or take a gap year and then re-sit, if the university will accept that. That's for you to find out, but perhaps it would be better if you get your head down and pass the first time?"

"I hope you know what you're saying, Theodore. I'm not sure I'm happy watching Justin jet off to countries that grow the damn drugs he smokes."

Theo could not help himself, and laughed out loud. "You've got to cut the umbilical cord; he's twenty-one. Maybe if you treated him more like an adult you'd both get on better."

"You've hardly been father of the year," Joanna shrieked in his face.

Theo pressed his hands together, mulling over his thoughts. His silence was taken as part of his usual antagonistic repertoire, which pushed Joanna into one of her acrid rants about how he had shamed her and deserted the family, just because he had become obsessed with sex with young women. Did he know how that made her feel? Well yes he did after all the years of punishment he had sustained from her and Justin, he thought quietly to himself.

Justin scraped his chair back and announced he needed a lift to the train station once he had packed his belongings to return to his university room.

When he returned with his over-stuffed duffle bag and rucksack slung over his shoulder, Joanna picked up her car keys and handbag and signalled for everyone to leave. Theo stood beside the car and held out his hand to Justin, who stared at it before tentatively reaching out. The weakness of the contact disheartened Theo, and he wanted more so he tapped the back of Justin's hand.

"Good luck. Be sure to let me know how you get on."

"Sure."

Joanna mumbled something before climbing into the driver's seat. Neither of them looked in his direction as they pulled out and drove away.

He turned around and looked up at the house, feeling a twinge of sadness as images of a past family life flashed across his gaze. Had he left it too late to turn things around?

Chapter 25

Summer sun scorched Alice's shoulders as she walked up to the main entrance of the hospice. The resident dirty grey pigeons hopped from branch to branch in the cherry tree on the front lawn. She inhaled deeply before buzzing to be let in.

Classical music was piped into the reception area, calming the atmosphere. The receptionist greeted Alice with her broad, warm smile; the whiteness of her teeth accentuated by the blood-red lipstick and black skin.

"Good morning," she said brightly. "Here's your volunteer badge. You can go through to the day room, they're expecting you."

Alice pinned the badge to her dress and wandered into the day room where she was greeted by Hope, who was running a painting session. She introduced Alice to Alan, who suffered with motor neuron disease. His speech was faltered and periodically incoherent, but his eyes sparkled. He wanted to go into the garden.

Alice quashed an overriding sense of pity; knowing it was not what people like Alan sought. With a cautiousness she had not expected to feel so deeply, she wheeled him outside to find a shady spot to sit in. How could she moan about her life when Alan was clearly still absorbing any positive aspect the day could present him with.

For the first time in a long while, she felt she was doing something useful as she crushed some fresh lavender between his hands and raised them up to his nose for him to inhale the fragrant odour.

The neurosurgeon studied Theo's MRI scan whilst tapping a pen against his chin. Beads of sweat trickled down Theo's spine, plastering his shirt to his skin.

"I'd like to do a biopsy of the tumour, see what we're dealing with. Any questions?"

The mechanical attitude of the consultant took Theo by surprise. He had imagined that anyone working in that field would talk in hushed tones, and look with pitying eyes at the patient before them.

"Any ideas what kind of tumour it is? Do I have long to live?"

"With your signs and symptoms, we could be looking at high-grade astrocytes tumour, but only the biopsy will tell us. Sometimes it's in part of the brain which is difficult to reach without the risk of damage. Ultimately, the decision about treatment is up to you. You have the choice of surgery, chemotherapy, and radiotherapy. And as for your last question, for that I have no answer. Try not to dwell on that."

Easier said than done, Theo thought as he stood up to leave, eager to get away from the sterility of the hospital.

The sun dried the perspiration on his face in seconds as he walked towards the underground station. People bustled and jostled passed him, unaware he was walking through a personal quagmire and developing a dense fog in his head. He felt they should see it, somehow, and treat him with more care.

The air in the underground was thin and drying, exacerbating the waves of nausea buffering him. Sections of the consultant's soliloquy rumbled through his mind. Was he being truthful or was he hiding the fact he had little time left? Could the tumour really be treated?

On the tube, people around him were unsmiling, trapped in their own worlds, as though each were encased in an impenetrable glass bauble. How many people, he wondered, were sitting there with their own life sentence hanging over them? How many of them were about to lose someone they love, or lose a job, or get divorced? Life was so full of uncertainties.

His train of thought led him to realize how alone he was. His parents were dead, he was an only child, and he was single. Then there was Joanna and Justin. Should he keep them informed of his health issue, give them chance to adjust to his situation, or should he leave it so when he is lying on a hospital bed, wretched with pain and gaunt from the life-force being sucked out of him, he passes away unnoticed.

He had not paid attention to where he was until he realised he had missed his stop and was close to Joanna's home. Without thinking, he jumped off the tube and headed for his past matrimonial home.

He arrived, sweating with heat and emotions, just as Joanna was watering the pots either side of the front door. She caught sight of him and straightened up.

"What on earth do you want?"

He bit his lip. "I was wondering if we could talk?"

She nodded, allowing him to walk up to her.

"So what can I do for you? Have you changed your mind about helping Justin?"

"Could we perhaps talk inside?"

Joanna paused, checking her watch. "Rory will be back soon, you'll have to be quick."

He followed her inside to the kitchen.

"I've got to marinate the prawns, but I can still listen to you."

Now that he was there, he was not sure what to say. Would she cry? Would she forgive him, and beg him to come back?

"I've just seen a consultant. They think I have a brain tumour. I'm having a biopsy."

"I hope you've made a will, Justin would welcome any funds." She watched him in the reflection of the window as she opened the bag of prawns and tipped them into the colander over the sink. "Of course I'm sorry for your situation, but it may be benign."

Theo felt deflated by her reaction but he recognized she had stopped loving him the day the incriminating photos appeared in the tabloid newspaper. What was he expecting?

"Are you shocked, or just hiding it well?"

Joanna rinsed the prawns before tipping them into a bowl and covering them with sweet chilli sauce. She placed them in the fridge and turned around to face him.

"If we were still happily married, I would have been devastated, believe me. But the part of my heart which was dedicated to you turned to stone the day you so publically cheated on me." She folded her arms and looked at the floor. "I loved you so much once, but now I'm finding it difficult to even care for you."

"You were challenging to live with at times, Joanna. So much so, in fact, that I wasn't sure if you loved me or not. Your nagging was relentless at times."

"*You* turned me into a nag."

Theo held his hands out. "Please, let's stop. I didn't come here to argue or rake up the past. I'm feeling vulnerable."

"I'm sorry you feel that way, but you've come to the wrong person. Perhaps you shouldn't have treated that woman in France so badly."

"You read my columns?"

"I was intrigued. She sounded a bit wet for you, but she obviously cared for you. It's a shame you treat people with such distain. All your wounds are self-inflicted." She retrieved a tin of sweetcorn from the cupboard. "Shame on you, Theodore."

"You know me, thoughtless where others are concerned, but the column was a success." He paused to rub his temple. "On reflection, I don't need anyone really, the consultant just got inside my head momentarily. Sorry to have troubled you."

"By the way, Justin is working hard, in case you were wondering," she said before turning her back on him to prepare a salad. Theo left the house, closing the door quietly behind him.

On arriving home he was greeted by Rufus who seemed more affectionate than normal.

"Can you sense I'm ill?" he asked, bending down to stroke the cat. "They say dogs can smell cancer, perhaps you can too."

After a traumatic day, he felt a whiskey was in order. He poured a large measure and wandered to the lounge.

Being an old Victorian house, it was fresh in the summer and retained the heat in the winter. He sat on the cool leather sofa, swirling his drink around the glass, watching the oily-looking film coating the sides of the glass as the light illuminated the amber colour of the liquid. Something Joanna said was whirling around his mind on a loop, as Alice's face kept appearing before him.

Suddenly, he was pricked by an alien feeling: guilt. He felt wobbly, sick, and deflated as the feeling began rusting his pristine armour.

Getting up, he moved to his writing desk and riffled around in a drawer until he found the sheet of paper with Alice's contact details. He returned to his seat, turning the paper over and over between his fingers whilst he finished his drink. *What should I do?*

Theo woke up on the sofa with Rufus curled up on his lap and the scrap of paper on the floor. The empty glass sat on the coffee table next to the half-drunk bottle. His dream of Alice's presence was so intense, his first action was to look around for her.

As he stirred, Rufus stretched out and arched his back before jumping off his lap. Theo reached down and picked up the piece of paper then took out his mobile. He wondered whether a text would be preferable as it would save him the embarrassment of her putting the phone down on him, which he fully expected after giving her a false number.

His fingers hovered over the keys as doubts crowded his mind. Returning his mobile to his top pocket, he moved to the kitchen to hunt out a cigarette.

Three cigarettes remained in the crumpled packet. He studied the white sticks before shoving the packet back in the drawer; deciding to save them for a time when only a smoke would do.

He tried to banish thoughts of Alice by reading a turgid novel he had to review for the newspaper. The book failed in its magic, and Alice insisted on remaining firmly in his mind. "That's it," he declared to Rufus, stomping back to the kitchen whilst taking the mobile out of his top pocket.

Chapter 26

Alice froze at Theo's text message. The combination of anti-depressants and volunteering had enabled her to push thoughts of him into the recesses of her mind, so his message had the potential to upset her new-found, albeit delicate equilibrium.

Columns about the writers' retreat had ceased, and he had returned to book reviewing, so her fear of reading further details about her failings and her miserable life had been erased. With newfound friends at St. Lydia's, she had learnt to treasure her life, so did she really want to reconnect with the man who hurt and ridiculed her, assisting her spiralling descent into the black hole of depression?

Outside the window, a howling wind ripped the first weak leaves from the trees. Summer was being eclipsed by the early fingers of autumn, but the afternoons were still balmy. She was too distracted to write, or even sit down, so she picked up her mobile and read his text for the umpteenth time.

I don't know if you want to talk to me, but if you do you can text me on this number; the right number this time, sorry. I'd dearly like to meet up, if you feel able. However, I totally understand if the thought repulses you. Theo.

Her initial thought was he had run out of material for the newspaper and was initiating contact to garner more fodder to make his readers giggle. Part of her wanted to see him to tell him how much his actions had hurt her. But she was not going to rush into making a decision that could negatively affect her depression. She took heed in the fact that she had loved unwisely in the past, and now was a time for caution, not hot-headed bravado.

Justin was keen to see his father with the news of his academic situation; the incentive of finances for a gap year had encouraged him to peruse the curriculum with more than a cursory glance. On ringing the doorbell, he envisaged the look of delight on his father's face.

"Hell Dad, you look like crap."

"Nice to see you too."

They shook hands limply as Justin stepped inside, running his gaze over his father's drawn face. Dark shadows inhabited the space under his eyes, which had lost their edgy sparkle, and he had become unattractively thin. His linen shirts hung on him like damp washing on a line.

Justin chose not to dwell on his father's appearance and proceeded to inform him of his achievement; not a high one by any means, he had just scraped a pass.

"It was your promise of money that helped. I hope it wasn't a lie," he said, eyeing him suspiciously.

"Of course it wasn't a lie. I know I haven't been the greatest father, but even that would be a low blow."

Theo fetched the bottle of whisky and two glasses, then they proceeded to drink to Justin's success before the issue of money was raised. Theo disliked Justin's overt obsequiousness just to meet his own agenda, but he went along with it. What else could he do? He had helped to form the man before him, so he could expect little else.

He watched Justin rummaged around in his rucksack, searching for his bank book, noticing his unkempt, bohemian quality, which undoubtedly attracted the women he was never short of. He was also insouciant in his attitude towards life, which Theo put down to his habit of smoking skunk, but now believed it was a trait inherited from Joanna; something she portrayed in her younger years, before marriage soured her. He felt a pang of envy towards them both.

Justin's savings amounted to one and a half thousand pounds, which Theo suspected had been topped up by Joanna. But he cared not; he just wanted Justin to enjoy life before he became burdened with a career, marriage, and children. And it was perhaps for that reason Joanna had failed to mention his own health issue and he decided to do the same.

"What are your plans?"

"I want to leave as soon as possible, but I haven't worked out an itinerary. I want to take in India, of course."

Theo smiled to himself, imagining Joanna's sentiments to that news. Silence consumed the pair as he wrote a cheque; the pretence was getting harder to maintain. He noticed Justin biting the skin around his thumbnail and tapping his foot impatiently on the floor.

"There's the money as promised, with a bit extra for unforeseen circumstances."

"Cool, thanks. I'd better be off now, Mum's taking me out for a celebration meal." He displayed no shame in revealing the evening's plan, from which Theo was excluded. Money was clearly more important than their relationship, making Theo's heart shrivel. He hoped his son had a better life mapped out than his own tawdry attempt.

At the front door, he made an awkward attempt to give Justin a hug, but it was so alien to them both, it failed to convey Theo's continued love of his son as they merely bumped shoulders. Justin did not turn back to wave as he reached the pavement, leaving Theo to watch him disappear down the road with the pronounced bounce of youth in his step. Theo wondered whether that was the last time they would ever meet.

Alice returned home following a shift at the hospice. The hours had given her the opportunity to reflect on the loneliness eating away at her soul, resigning her to her state of spinsterhood for the rest of her life, but perhaps she could include Theo as a friend. Just a friend.

She poured a glass of wine before retrieving her mobile from her bag. She re-read his text then composed a reply.

I was surprised to hear from you, especially after reading what you really thought of me. Against my own council I would like to meet up to discuss your actions. We should meet somewhere neutral. Alice.

She hesitated before pressing SEND. Her heart racing, she took to wandering around the flat, wondering whether he would reply that evening, or play it cool and reply the next day, if indeed at all.

Half an hour later, as she sat nursing her second glass of wine, she received a text.

Great to hear from you. Sorry you read my columns, yes we should discuss them. How about tomorrow night at seven at The Partridge pub in Bethnal Green? Theo.

After a quick reply to confirm the arrangement, she walked to her wardrobe to peruse her clothes. His ascorbic and mocking comments rattled around her mind as she sifted through her clothes, discarding each item with his laughter ringing in her ears.

Alice popped the three tiny white pills into her mouth and swallowed them with a mouthful of tepid coffee. It had become her morning ritual after eating some toast. The medication was finally working, but it wasn't a magic solution. She still needed to work at having a more positive outlook, and her role at St. Lydia's was aiding her. She still could not face calling the counselling service, feeling unworthy of their help, and fearful of hearing her thoughts out loud making them real. She suspected she would look the fool she felt she was.

She planned to pass the hours before meeting Theo by perfecting her look; she had even booked an appointment with a hairdresser. She wanted to look the best she could so she did not resemble the pitiful specimen he had written about.

Theo sat opposite the consultant to discuss the results of the biopsy. The consultant took off his glasses and opened up the conversation with the results, followed by the treatments available to him.

Theo heard the conversation as though he had sea shells clamped over his ears. He felt dizzy as the consultant listed the choice of treatments, finally offering him the service of a specialist nurse. When the consultant stopped speaking, he waited for Theo to speak, but his tongue was stuck to the roof of his dry mouth. They batted thoughts back and forth before the consultant brusquely handed him some leaflets and the number for the nurse before dismissing him.

He travelled home on autopilot, not registering the weather, the time, or the people around him. He had worried for almost a year that the headaches may be a sign of some underlying condition, but he had been too busy to see his doctor. *No*, he thought, *not busy . . . afraid.*

He remembered his mother being ill in bed at home, the smell of decaying flesh clinging to the walls of the house as she got sicker. As her demise progressed to the final stages, the smell was replaced by the cloying headiness of death. And after she died, the house was never the same and neither was his father.

Theo poured hot water on a teabag in a mug as he remembered returning home from boarding school one afternoon to find his father's lifeless body hanging from the bannister. He had sensed something was wrong as soon as he opened the front door; the smell of death had become pungent once more. The morbid silence ringing in the atmosphere of the house was thick with unsaid sentiments, and unforgotten pain.

His father had left a suicide note to explain that life without his wife was meaningless and unbearable; Theo had only ever played a minor role in his life, so his father did not stop to consider whether suicide was the only option to him. In his eyes, he had nothing left to give or receive from another, including his only child.

From that day on, Theo was damaged. Not only did he inherit wealth, he also inherited a fear of life and of loving another so much that living became unbearable without them. He did not want a child of his own, but Joanna had a different opinion, and she won. He was a constant loser in his life.

Chapter 27

Groups of smokers stood outside The Partridge pub when Alice arrived ten minutes later than scheduled. Her nose wrinkled up as she weaved her way through them.

Inside, music from the jukebox travelled through the air. A couple of portly men were propping up the bar, chatting to a young barmaid who was stifling a yawn.

Alice scanned the semi-dark room and saw Theo reading a paper at a table for two. She straightened her back and walked towards him.

"Theo."

He looked up, crumpling the paper in his lap. "Alice, you look different . . . I mean great."

"Hello, you look rather under the weather, not the swaggering flamboyant man I met in France."

"I'm clearly not aging well. You look well, have you lost weight?"

"No, I'm exactly the same. I've just had my hair cut."

Theo stood up, motioning to the other chair. "I'll get you a drink. Red wine?"

Alice sat down, nodding. Watching him walk away, she noticed his walk was slower, and his hair had lost its lustre. He had an air of quiet sadness about him; was he chagrined? Surely not.

He returned with her wine, and they sipped their drinks in silence, waiting for the storm to begin. Alice could wait no longer.

"Why did you lie in France and write such awful things about me and the others? You were vitriolic."

"I'm a journalist and it was my job to write about the retreat. My articles are always ascorbic, no matter what I write about, I'm afraid. I lied because none of you would have talked to me if you knew my reason for being there, which would have negated the premise of my columns."

"And was sleeping with me part of the plan too?"

"No, that was a mistake."

Alice winced aloud, picking up her glass to hide her discomfort.

"I didn't mean it like that, Alice. I meant that I shouldn't have slept with anyone. That was out of line."

"Why do you say that? If you think it'll placate me, then you're wrong. Were you acting like that because of your divorce?" Her voice was louder than she intended, making the other patrons turn around. She didn't care.

"It has nothing to do with the divorce, or you, come to that. I'm a messed up individual. Many women have tried to sort me out, believe me."

Alice rolled her eyes. "Why did you invite me here? Do you need more laughs for your paper?" She was drinking faster than normal.

"It's bizarre, but I found myself missing your company and your calming influence."

Her eyebrows arched, then memories of France flooded back. "You lied when you slept with me, when you held me after love-making, and you lied to me every waking moment. How can I trust you now? Why would I want to, quite frankly?"

"I'm not asking us to carry on from our French days, I'm only asking for your friendship and companionship."

Alice emptied her glass, placing it down rather noisily on the table. "And how do you see this friendship panning out? How would we conduct ourselves?"

"We both enjoy wining and dining, and we both love reading. I think we'd find plenty to talk about. I'd pay for everything, naturally."

"So now you're treating me like an escort. Are you going to pay me enough to sleep with you too?"

"Don't be ridiculous, I offered to pay for our outings because I have very little else to spend my money on, and I'm clearly richer than you."

"How so?" Alice's indignation prickled the hairs on the back of her neck.

"My clothes are a better quality than yours, for starters. Look Alice, why can't you just accept my offer with no questions asked?"

"Because when I took you at face value last time, you besmirched me in your articles. You *ridiculed* me about my prowess between the sheets," she whispered hoarsely.

"How many times do I have to apologize for that? You weren't supposed to see them; I'm not sure how you have, really." He took several large mouthfuls of drink, looking at her constantly over the rim of the glass. "If you have a full and interesting social life then I'll leave you alone. But if, like me, you'd like a friend in your life, then accept my offer."

"I would have thought you were inundated with friends."

"I was when I was married, but then I discovered they were more loyal to Joanna than me. Plus, my other acquaintances were authors who turned away after I panned their novels." He finished his drink then shook the empty glass at her.

"I shouldn't, really," she replied, uncertain of what she wanted.

"How about we go for a meal? There's a great Thai restaurant not far from here."

"I think we may have said all there is to say for one evening."

Theo's shoulder's dipped. "Have I lost my charm?"

"I seem to remember in France, Zoe found you attractive. I'm sure if you hang around the bar, you'll find some young thing to pick up, eventually."

"That's not what I want, but I won't force you to do something you don't want to do. I'd like to give you my correct and full contact details," he said, handing her a business card.

Alice took it and popped it in her bag without looking at it.

"Can we do this again?" he asked.

"Perhaps," she replied, monitoring her voice, as she rose and turned away.

Her mind was numb as she strolled through Victoria Park. She was oblivious of the swans cruising around the lake, and the young lovers kissing and holding hands.

Her flat seemed lonelier that evening. Programmes on the TV bored her, and she lacked concentration to read a book. She pulled Theo's card out of her bag and stared at it. He was a hard man to read, yet she was allowing him to seep back into her life, even though her heart had metastasized with a disease he had propagated.

The wine had made her drowsy, and as her head sank into the pillow, her eyes closed allowing her mind to be engulfed by the hollow darkness of sleep.

Theo finished typing a demolishing book review and sent it to Charles before leaning back in his chair, balancing precariously on the two back legs, as the emerging dawn chorus was waking the sleepy garden.

He had a fractious night's sleep as a myriad of thoughts flooded his mind regarding the medical options open to him. He was not sure he wanted to spend his last possible months attending gruelling chemo or radiotherapy sessions, but he wondered if he would think differently if he were in a relationship. Perhaps a loved one would urge him to fight on.

When the phone rang, he grabbed it quickly.

"Hello," he said brightly.

"Goodness Theodore, you obviously weren't expecting it to be me," said Joanna.

"Not exactly. What can I do for you?"

"It's more what I can do for you. Justin's leaving for his trip next week and I thought you might want to come and have dinner with us, seeing as your situation's a bit tricky."

Theo laughed dryly. "Is that how you see my situation?"

"Don't test me, Theodore. Now do you want to come or not?"

"Is Justin aware of my health issue?"

"No, I saw no reason to upset him before his adventure."

"Fair enough. It would be lovely to see him before he leaves."

"Okay, tomorrow evening at seven thirty. Don't be late."

"You know me," he quipped, but all he heard was the click on the other end.

Alice arrived at the hospice to be greeted by Sadie.

"I hate to ask you this, but would you sit with Alan. The doctor believes he may be close to dying, and I'm sure your presence would be comforting. Do you think you can cope?"

Alice swallowed hard. "I think so."

"You don't have to, you're a volunteer. It's just Alan enjoyed his time with you immensely, and he's got no family."

Sadie led her to Alan's room, situated at the end of the corridor. On the front of his door was a photograph of Alan as a young man, smiling on a ski slope. They entered quietly to find a nurse sitting at his bedside. Soft sunshine radiated into his room, bathing the walls with a soft yellow light. The melodic tones of Mozart, Alan's favourite composer, shifted through the air, and a lavender candle flickered on his bedside table.

The nurse stood up and gently told Alan she was leaving and that Alice would be sitting with him. On hearing her name, his eyelids twitched but remained closed.

Alice settled in the chair next to his bed and watched Sadie and the nurse retreat from the room. Suddenly she felt a vast responsibility on her shoulders, knowing she needed to offer Alan the stillness and companionship he required in perhaps his last hours.

She gently took his hand in hers. It felt cold and small, like a child who had been playing in the snow without wearing gloves. With her other hand, she opened the book of Ted Hughes poetry and began quietly reading aloud.

Every now and then, the fragrant odour of lavender drifted under her nose, reminding her of France and of her mother. Too many emotions crowded her mind. Blinking rapidly, she blotted back a tear as she refocused on being there for Alan.

He made a rattling sound as he breathed, and she noticed a purple, blotchy, mottling effect on his hands. After a while she felt what tiny strength he had in the hand she was holding dissipate. She scrutinized his chest to watch for any movement, but saw nothing. She sat with him for a few minutes, which felt like hours, before pressing the red button to summon the nurse.

The nurse arrived and checked him for signs of life, then opened the window. Alice frowned.

"I leave the window open for the soul to pass through. It's a habit I picked up on the elderly acute medical ward in hospital, when I was a student nurse. We used to leave a flower on their chest too."

Alice was aware of her eyes prickling with tears, and when the nurse checked how she was feeling, a couple of fat tears spilled over and rolled down her cheeks. She swallowed hard.

"There's nothing to be ashamed of, a touching tear is a fitting way to say goodbye to one of our guests, and I'm sure he appreciated your company," she said, placing her hand on Alice's shoulder. "You can talk to the counsellor if that would help."

Having declined a chat with the counsellor, Alice was at home feeling washed out and disorientated. Gazing at the blue-grey sky, she imagined Alan's spirit floating up there, and thought he would get on well with her mother. The thought brought a fleeting smile to her lips, imaging the pair swapping memories about their youths.

She warmed up a tin of tomato soup and buttered a bread roll, wondering what Theo was doing and if he was thinking of her.

Chapter 28

Joanna had decided against a meal in public, lest anyone she knew saw them all together. Instead, she paid caterers to provide the meal at her home, so all she had to do was serve it. Whilst she pottered in the kitchen, Theo and Justin sat in the lounge watching the news on TV. The sound irked her.

"You're not watching TV all night," she said, striding into the room and hitting the power button on the remote. "It may be a while before you meet again, so why don't you talk to one another."

"We've got nothing to say," replied Justin, who was slouching on the sofa, his long legs arching out in front of him like the legs of a giant spider.

"He's not interested in me now that he has the money," added Theo, before draining his glass.

"Can't you two not bicker just for one evening?"

"It's the only way we know to communicate, I just can't relate to the archaic way Dad sees the world. We're different generations."

"In the real world people do talk to one another regardless of their generation rating. Perhaps when you join the human race and get a job, you'll discover this for yourself." Theo was already tiring of the evening and they had not even begun the meal.

"I haven't gone to all this hard work for you two to be disagreeable."

"You haven't done any work, the caterers did it for you," Justin grunted.

Theo spluttered then roared with laughter, leaving Joanna red-faced in the doorway telling them to go to the dining room. They rose slowly from their seats and dawdled to the next room, neither person feeling hungry.

A floral centrepiece which Joanna had collected from the florist that morning sat on the dining table. She placed herself at the head, with the men sitting opposite one another. Only three places were set.

"No Rory tonight?" asked Theo.

"No, he thought it would be less stressful without him. He's gone to his club."

"Less stressful for him, more like," chipped in Justin.

Joanna tutted, scooping some crab mousse onto her fork. The men followed suit and Justin wrinkled up his nose.

"I think I'm going to return from travelling as a vegetarian," he declared, picking up a sprig of watercress and folding it into his mouth. He chewed it like a cow eating grass.

"You'd better bloody not. I'm not cooking two meals every evening," she said firmly.

"I won't be living here, hopefully. I'll rent a place of my own."

"With what money?" Joanna asked.

"Something will sort itself out. If not, you two can help me. Let's face it, dick-face Rory hasn't enjoyed me being here, has he?"

Theo allowed a smile to creep across his lips.

"I'm curious, what attracted you to Dad?" asked Justin.

"He was a charismatic and mysterious man, the quintessential enigma."

"Your mother means I was a challenge. She had to have me no matter what."

"Don't big yourself up, Theodore, you did a fair amount of charming me at the time, I seem to remember."

"But what on earth made you marry and have a kid? You have nothing in common. Why didn't you just shag and separate."

"Don't be so uncouth, Justin, I raised you better than that," she said tersely.

"Hell, when are you going to see me as a man, and not a child?"

"You'll always be my child, which means I can always keep you in your place."

"No wonder I want to get a way for a year."

Theo was making strenuous efforts to keep the peace by not taking sides or adding sarcastic quips here and there. He made a banal comment about how lovely the crab mousse was.

"Are you saying that because I didn't make it?"

"Can't I say anything without you misconstruing what I mean?"

"I don't know what I was thinking inviting you for dinner. If you weren't ill I wouldn't have bothered. You've spoilt the whole evening."

"Dad's ill?"

Joanna turned to Justin as though forgetting he was in the room.

"Are you going to answer me then, or do I have to pry it out of loose-lipped Mum?"

"We didn't want to worry you before your trip," Theo said quietly.

"Well now I've been made aware that you're ill, I might as well know what's wrong."

An ominous silence shrouded the group.

"Oh for pities sake, he's got a brain tumour," she said in a strident voice.

He turned to Theo. "You weren't going to tell me? Yet you could die whilst I'm miles away." Justin threw his cutlery down on the bone china plate, chipping it in the process.

Joanna was about to chastise him, but Theo raised his hand. "I'm sorry, Son, perhaps it was a thoughtless thing to do, but I did have your best interests at heart."

"You don't know what's best for me. You hardly bloody know me at all. You're both such shit parents." Justin stood up sharply, his chair toppling backwards to the floor as he left the room. The clattering sound made Joanna shriek.

"Look what you've done," she yelled at Theo. "I think you should leave."

He didn't need asking twice. Pulling his jacket from the back of his chair, he made his way to the door. "I'll call him in a couple of days; give him time to calm down."

"Oh do what you want; you always do." Joanna stood up, pushing passed him and stomping upstairs.

If Theo had any positive feelings left about the house, they had been totally obliterated. He couldn't wait to get back to Bethnal Green.

Descending the dirty stone steps into the underground, he was met by a blast of dusty warm air as a train pulled into the station. He sat down and watched his reflection in the window, seeing he had aged over the course of the evening.

He was not tired, or drunk, and he was still hungry. He thought about calling in on Alice, but preferred the idea of grabbing a pizza on the way home and having it with a couple of beers in solitude.

Alice wiped away a tear as she sat in the doctor's surgery. Her last moments with Alan had taken their toll. The doctor spoke gently to her and told her she was proud of her progress.

"I don't see your tears for Alan as tears of depression," she said. "They're normal in the circumstances. Let's keep you on the same dose of medication and continue with what you're doing. You still haven't made an appointment with the counsellor, I see."

Alice shrugged. "What I'm doing at the moment is working for now."

"Well remember it's there for you, but I'm very proud of what you're doing."

It was good for Alice to receive some positive affirmations. It lifted her mood, so that even the drizzle did not perturb her as she walked home.

On approaching her block of flats, she saw a lone hunched-over figure standing by the entrance. Moving closer she saw it was Theo wearing a rain mac with the collar turned up. She paused slightly, before pushing her shoulders back.

"Hello, Alice. I hope you don't mind me dropping by unannounced."

Remembering the positive words of her doctor, she relaxed her furrowed brow and smiled. "Not at all, come in."

They strolled in together and took the stairs up to her flat.

"Tea or coffee?" she offered.

"A coffee would be great, thanks." He sat down at the kitchen table whilst she made the drinks.

"How have you been keeping?" she asked, keeping her back to him.

"Not bad, but I had a disastrous meal with my son and my ex last night."

"Do you often dine together?"

"Hell no. Justin's going travelling for a year so it was a farewell meal, really."

"So why was it such a failure?" she said, putting the mugs on the table before sitting opposite him.

"I think just being in the same room as my ex sparks off old tensions, and Justin has his mother's temperament."

Alice had no experience of being married let alone being a parent. She had only ever lived with her mother. "And perhaps some of yours too," she smiled. "Families can be insanely complex."

"You don't have any children, do you?" he asked.

She shook her head, lifting the mug to her lips.

"Do you have any regrets?"

"Ones you'd like to publish, perhaps?"

"I deserve that. No, I'm being genuine, if you can believe me."

She smiled briefly. "My life hasn't turned out as I imagined, but then who gets all they desire?"

"Some people have more opportunities than others. I had a privileged life financially."

"And did that add to your ability to attain happiness?"

"I'm not sure what happiness feels like. What happy I did achieve was due to me working hard."

"Did you not feel happiness when you got married, or at the birth of your son?"

"I hoped that marriage would bring me that elusive emotion, but Joanna had a different view on happiness. Happiness for her was in the materialistic sphere, a view I don't share."

"And fatherhood?"

Theo paused and sipped his coffee, no longer feeling like a journalist but rather like the prey. *So this is what it feels like.*

"Fatherhood was foisted upon me, I didn't seek it out. However, once I met the baby, I was totally enamoured with him, until he turned a teenager. Or perhaps it was until I left his mother."

Alice heard the splinters of pain in his voice, snagging her heart. She felt she had very little to offer him, not like being with Alan, where words of comfort were easy to find.

They both stared into the middle-distance, both suffering various degrees of pain.

"I was wondering whether I could take you out for dinner this evening, unless you're busy." His eyes glided over her face briefly.

Her frown lines deepened. "Perhaps."

"Great, I'll meet you at eight. We can eat late like we did in France. I'll leave you in peace now," he said as he got up and made his way to her front door. "Don't you miss having a garden?"

"I'm happy to use the local parks for my contact with nature."

He nodded swiftly then left.

Once alone, Alice tidied away the cups and revisited their conversation. There was a profound sadness to him she had not noticed in France. She wondered whether it was a new acquisition, or whether it had been present in France but he had hidden it well behind clouds of cigarette smoke and deceit. She then wondered whether her own pain was as visible to others, and whether pity was their overall sentiment towards her.

Theo arrived to collect her dead on at eight o'clock. His eyes lingered on her longer than he intended; the clinging crossover dress enhanced her curvy figure, and her wavy, wild hair, tinged with a smattering of grey, gave her the air of a bohemian artist. She was the total opposite to Joanna's ironing-board figure, and long, perfectly straight, dyed blond hair.

They walked in silence, strolling along the uneven pavement with their arms occasionally brushing up against one another as they once did in France.

Once seated in the restaurant, Theo ordered a bottle of chilled rosé wine and gave a cursory glance to the menu.

"I'm sorry I wrote about the university incident. No one would know it was you."

"That's not the point, I knew. You violated my confidence and pushed the incident into the foreground of my mind. I felt humiliated all over again." She dug her nails into the palms of her hands.

"I see that now. In fact, I see a lot of my misguided actions littering my past. But it's too late for me to rectify many of those things now."

"Is that what you're doing with me now: rectifying things?"

"I suppose it is."

"So it's not too late for you to do this for your other victims."

"Is that how you see yourself, as a victim?"

"I've been a victim most of my life thanks to certain people, mostly men. But of late, I've changed my outlook, and I'm grabbing life by the collar and making it mine."

"What spurred the change?"

"I've been volunteering, and it's taught me to appreciate what I have, even though it's not all I want."

The waiter arrived with their steaming food, which was delicately fragranced with ginger, jasmine, and lemon grass. Alice inhaled the fragrant mélange as she ate, occasionally glancing at Theo.

"I hope one day you can consider me as a friend," he finally said.

"If after we've met a few times and there's nothing written about me in the paper, I may start trusting you again."

Theo smiled.

"What happened to you to make you so bitter and dismissive of other people's feelings?" she asked faintly.

Theo took a deep breath and gave her an insight into his childhood and the fate of his parents. By the time he had finished, their meals were cold.

"You had a tough start, and I'm sorry. I understand where you're coming from now, but it's still not an excuse to trounce other people's lives."

Theo tentatively reached across the table and took her hand. She liked the familiar but slightly forgotten touch. Her feelings merged to the surface like the frothy head on a pint of Guinness, and after a few minutes, she allowed herself to squeeze his hand gently.

Both found their appetites diminished, only picking at the rest of their meal.

"Why don't we go back to mine for coffee? And no, that isn't a euphemism," he smiled, crinkling the thinning skin around his eyes.

As they meandered back, Theo took her hand and interlinked his fingers with hers. It was very reminiscent of walking back to the chateaux from the bar, without the anticipation of sex intermingled with alcohol and the stench of Gauloises.

"Were you ever in love with Joanna, or just trying to fulfil a utopian fantasy?"

Theo looked down at her, frowning. "I loved her of sorts, but I think love is something different in each stage of life. It can't be compared to a love in a different phase."

"You have a warped way of looking at things."

"Perhaps I only dare say what other people think. We're here," he said, opening a wrought-iron gate for her to pass through.

Chapter 29

There was a citrusy, musky scent in Theo's house which reminded Alice of his aftershave.

He showed her into the lounge before moving to the kitchen to make the coffee. Alice wandered along the bookshelves lining two of the walls, running her finger along some leather bound classics. There were hardback first editions of authors whom she had never heard of. She suspected many of them would be signed.

She was still standing by the bookshelves when he arrived with a pot of coffee and two mugs.

"I've been given most of those to review. I save a fortune in reading-matter."

"Doesn't reviewing take the pleasure out of reading?"

"Not always. If the book is riveting then I'll say so and say why. But if it's a torturous read, then it's a chore, but the review is somehow more fun to write."

She found that easy to believe.

"Come and sit down, the books will still be there another day."

"Ah, but will I?"

He offered a lopsided smile, knowing he was not the one in control this time; they were no longer in France.

Sitting on the sofa together, he reached out and rested his arm along the back, letting his hand hover near the nape of her neck. He knew it was a juvenile move but that made it all the more perfect. What would have happened if he had met her instead of Joanna? Perhaps he would have been cured of his apathy towards others, and been a more amenable person in the process.

Neither of them was prepared for the sound of the doorbell, which increased in persistency. With an irritated sigh, Theo got up to answer it. Alice heard his voice then that of a woman's, although she could not hear what was being said. The woman's voice rose before the clip-clopping sound of heels echoed in the hallway.

"I thought you must have a woman here. Why else would you not be interested in the plight of *our* son?" Joanna said tersely. "You'll have to conduct your evening of carnal entertainment another time, Theodore has more important things to do," she said directly to Alice.

Alice remained seated, dumbfounded by the attack and Theo's silence. She was also stunned to see what a beautiful and elegant woman Joanna was. Theo had never alluded to her beauty, but any fool could see her natural poise and grace, her sleek blond hair cutting sharply over her shoulders, and a large diamond and emerald necklace adorning her swan-like neck. Her steely eyes never flinched from Alice, forcing her to move.

She rose, clutching her handbag tightly and hoping Theo would say something, anything, to prevent her from leaving. In what he did not say, he said so much.

Blinking back tears, she left the house, knowing that whatever she and Theo had was over. Well and truly over.

"You didn't have to speak to her like that," snapped Theo. "She's a sweet woman. None of this is her fault."

"Ah, so you see her as sweet, do you? So why didn't you stand up for her? Maybe she's not quite slutty enough in the bedroom for you, otherwise you'd have chased me away, not her."

"I didn't chase her away, you did."

"But you didn't stop me. Anyway, I don't care about her, I'm worried about Justin. He's supposed to leave in two days and he's disappeared, leaving me this note." She handed the rough-edged scrap of paper to Theo.

I've gone away as you both piss me off. I'm never treated as an adult, and even though you two hate one another, you still gang up on me. You both knew about Dad's illness but didn't think that I had a right to know. I can never win, and I'm tired of trying.

I'm still leaving the country, and I'm not telling you my plans, and this decision has made me feel happier than I've ever felt before. You two have worn me down, and made me feel inadequate. Everyone did drugs at uni, they just did it better than me so they didn't get caught. Once you two found out, it was the end of my life as I knew it.

Hopefully you two can stop meeting one another now that I've gone, and I hope Dad's health gets sorted, not that I'll find out.

Justin

"Well that's succinct," Theo said flatly. "I can't see what you want me to do?"

"Find him of course, you idiot. He could end up in a crack den for all we know, just out of spite. We should call the police."

"And say what exactly? That our adult son has decided to leave home and get a life. They'll laugh in our faces."

Joanna's face filled with rage. Her hand twitched, longing to slap his face. "I can see getting rid of your tart was pointless. You might as well call her back and jump into bed."

It was Theo's turn to feel the burn of anger. "What is it with you and my love life? You're about to get married and I don't complain, although I pity the man, but it leaves you no right to harp on about mine."

"Rory's left me. We argued interminably about Justin whom he had no sympathy for. I had to put Justin first."

"For what? I mean Justin's left you now, so you've lost both the men in your life for nothing."

"You're still around."

"Don't kid yourself. With Justin gone there really is no need for us to keep in contact. You managed without me for years, you can do it again."

"But I had Justin and Rory then. Besides, you're ill, you'll need me."

Theo ran his hand over the top of his head. "I can't be that person for you. I can't be there for you and I don't want you there for me either. I don't want you sitting at my bedside as I die, and I don't want you to be the last person I see. Sorry, Joanna, but that's how it is." He walked to the front door and opened it, waiting for her to leave.

"You'll change your tune. When you get worse and lose your hair, and whatever else may happen, you'll need me. See you sooner or later, Theodore," she said, strolling into the obscurity of the night.

Chapter 30

Two weeks had passed, and Alice was still reeling from Joanne's acerbic soliloquy, and feeling abandoned by Theo. Her depression had re-emerged fervently, turning her into a recluse. She remained in her pyjamas, mooching around the flat, and occasionally writing pages of morose prose before deleting it.

Periodically, she descended to the mailbox, successfully avoiding her neighbours by venturing out late in the evening.

On such an evening, Alice retrieved a hand written envelope from her mailbox. She touched the paper as though it could transmit who sent it. She opened it, and began reading.

Dear Alice,

I imagine you're surprised to hear from me. I wanted to reconnect with people on the retreat but Maggie would only give me your address thinking that you would be the person least likely to complain about her indiscretion.

How is your novel coming along? I had an agent read mine and they love it! But more of that later.

Do you see much of Theo? You two seemed a close item in France and I wondered whether it was a holiday romance or whether you're both still together?

I still think about Marlon. It did give me kudos in my local pub though, dating someone who killed themselves. They said I must have ruined him for other women and he knew he couldn't live without me. I didn't disagree with them, why would I?

Anyway, the agent I spoke of wants to meet me and I wondered if I could stay with you for a night? I thought we could hook up with Theo and go out for dinner in London. I don't get down there often, but if the agent takes me on, you may be seeing a lot of me! I've enclosed my e-mail account and mobile number, so you can contact me and tell me if it's okay.

Can't wait to see you,

Zoe x

Alice's heart sank. Did Zoe really just want to see Theo? *She can have him*, she thought to herself, *or she can fight Joanna for him, more like.* "I can stand back and watch the circus," she muttered aloud.

But if there was one thing her mother had taught her, it was to be accommodating to other people's needs above her own. Her mother's voice spoke to her as she e-mailed Zoe, offering her a room.

"Come in, Mr Edwards, take a seat," Doctor Stone said in her usual affable manner. "I understand from your consultant that you don't wish to undertake any treatment, only meds to manage your symptoms."

"Yes, and if you've called me in to try and change my mind, you've wasted your time, I'm afraid."

"I thought you could talk me through your reasoning. You're still a youngish, and most definitely an intelligent man; I'm at a loss as to why you don't want to pursue treatment."

"I've done my living and have left a messy trail to prove it. I've nothing to gain from living longer than I need to, and no one's depending on my longevity."

"You sound depressed."

"Not depressed, Doctor, I've lived unwisely, and taught my son to be an arrogant and egotistical man in the process. I leave no legacy except for my reviews and columns in the paper, for which I'm almost universally hated."

"I can't believe everyone hates you. You have a harsh view of yourself."

"It's justified. Perhaps you haven't read my work. Now if you have no other questions I'd like to go home and have a large whiskey, one of the few pleasures left to me now."

The phone was ringing as he opened his front door.

"You've slowed down a lot since France," she giggled. "It's Zoe. I bet you're surprised to hear from me."

"That's one verb I could use."

"Ever the charmer, I see. How have you been since the retreat? I've been tremendous, do you want to know why?"

He felt the question negated a response seeing as her previous one to him had been glossed over so artfully.

"I've got a meeting with an agent who loves my novel and I'm hoping they'll take me on. I'm coming down to London tomorrow. I'm staying with Alice, who gave me your number. I thought we could all go out for a meal or something; I might have something to celebrate."

Hearing Alice's name punched him straight in the stomach. "Great news about the agent, but I'm too busy to meet up."

"Then cancel whatever it is; I want to see you. I'll come round to your place and drag you out. You know I'm capable."

Theo summoned up fake enthusiasm and agreed before hanging up and pouring a large drink.

The intercom buzzer announced Zoe's arrival.

"Alice, you look fab! Love the new haircut, very *avant-garde*."

Alice smiled as she let her in. "Would you like a drink?"

"It's a fraction early for me, but what the heck. I'll have a gin and tonic, please."

"I did mean tea or coffee, but G&T it is."

She showed Zoe her mother's old room before moving to the kitchen to fix the drinks. It was odd to hear someone moving around the flat, especially coming from that room.

"Nice place, but don't you miss having an outside space?" Zoe asked.

"You're not the first person to ask me that," she replied with a wry smile. "I've lived here so long, I'm used to it."

"I'd feel so hemmed in. Mind you, you have a great view."

Alice nodded nonchalantly, giving Zoe her drink. "So tell me all about your meeting."

Zoe positively fizzed with excitement. "I've been bursting to tell you, it was amazing. The agent, Susie, had a contract drawn up for me, and she's already got a couple of publishers in mind. Erotica's the in thing, you know."

"Congratulations, you must be so excited."

"I am! I so want to go out and have some fun in London. Theo's coming here at seven, so we'd better get ready."

Alice swallowed hard. "Actually, I've got a migraine brewing. If you don't mind I'll have to stay here. You and Theo should have plenty to talk about." Alice hoped to see some disappointment in Zoe's eyes, but it was she who was disappointed.

"I'll have a shower and get ready in a minute, then I can leave you in peace," Zoe said, playing with the ice cubes in her glass. "You don't mind me dining alone with Theo, do you?"

"Of course not, we're not dating."

Alice sighed deeply as Zoe left to get ready. Her youthful buoyancy filled the flat like a large cloud of dry ice.

Chapter 31

Theo's face dropped when only Zoe appeared in the foyer.

"Just me, I'm afraid. Alice has got a migraine," she said, threading her arm through his and gazing up at him. "Where to?"

"I'm not wildly hungry. There's an Italian not far from here. Are you okay walking in those heels?" he asked.

"I remember you talking about a wine bar in Covent Garden when we were in France. Take me there and we'll see if we're hungry afterwards?"

Theo felt too weak to argue, so they headed for the underground, with Zoe clinging to him like a Russian vine strangling a sapling tree.

The Punch and Judy was teeming with people, some of them spilling out onto the balcony to watch the street entertainers in the square below.

"This is how I see London," she said excitedly. "If I lived here I'd be permanently exhausted from trying to keep up with the city. I'm going home tomorrow, but perhaps during the day you could take me to some art galleries. It would be an exquisite way to spend the day."

"We haven't even made it through this evening. Perhaps we should wait to see what tomorrow brings." He gently, but firmly, unhooked himself from her, before pushing his way through the crowd to get to the bar. He bought two large glasses of red wine then led her onto the balcony where there was standing room only.

"Here's to a success with my novel, and a thrilling time with you," she said, raising her glass.

Theo was distracted by the crowds milling around, the noise bubbling in his ears. He downed two large mouthfuls of wine before bending down and kissing her right on her mouth.

"I wasn't expecting that."

"Weren't you? I thought that's what you wanted when we were in France."

"You're so sure of yourself. I was more tempted by the younger body of Marlon, or have you forgotten him?"

"I've forgotten nothing of France."

"Meaning Alice, I take it. What happened to you two?"

"I just used her; she was easy to dupe."

"That's very harsh of you. I'm shocked."

"You shouldn't be; you know so little about me. I don't have a blemish-free track record."

"Who does?" she interjected. "Kiss me again, I rather liked it."

"Perhaps we should head back?"

"What's the rush? I quite like being amongst the artists and frivolous Londoners."

Theo threw back his head and laughed. "You're so young and innocent. It would be quite refreshing if it wasn't so ridiculous."

"Who are you calling ridiculous?" she snapped.

"Don't be so petulant, it spoils your beautiful face."

"So you acknowledge I'm beautiful."

"I never denied it."

She smiled and leant in to him, complicit in the understanding of the moment.

They finished their drinks, applauded the juggler, and headed off back to his place—food forgotten about.

Alice almost wished she did have a migraine so she could dose herself up with pain killers and sleep the evening away. Her thoughts kept drifting towards the delectable Zoe and Theo, enjoying food, wine, and conversation. She wondered whether Zoe would return.

Her omission to mention Theo's true vocation and the damning columns on the retreat to Zoe was now causing her concern. Had she led her into a trap where her follies would be printed in black and white for all to read and ridicule? She told herself Zoe was old enough to look after herself.

Theo took two glasses and the bottle of whiskey into the lounge where Zoe was ensconced on the leather sofa, her long legs draped along the seats. He expected to feel an urgency of excitement as he poured the drinks, and it was disconcerting to find he could not summon up the energy he knew she would demand.

"You look pensive," she said, taking a glass from him.

"Just feeling my age."

"You do look rather tired. Maybe I can make you feel younger," she said, lifting her legs for him to sit down, then placing them over his knees.

He closed his eyes and rested his head on the back of the sofa as visions of Alice floated before his eyes.

"I get the feeling the whiskey is the only thing that's going to warm me this evening," she said quietly. "I saw the disappointment in your face when I appeared without Alice. Does she know you're in love with her?"

Theo coughed. "What on earth makes you say that?"

"The time you spent with her in France, and the way you stare into the middle distance whenever I mention her name. A woman can tell these things. Here I am offering myself on the proverbial platter and you're not in the mood."

"I thought I was, and I may still be."

"Oh please, I do have some level of self-esteem. If she's the one you want why don't you just tell her?"

"Because she doesn't want me after I betrayed her trust."

Zoe shook her head and shrugged.

"She didn't tell you about my column in the newspaper?"

"No, but I'm intrigued. Tell me more."

He poured himself another drink, then clarified his real reason for going to France, and the tone of his columns. He hid nothing from her, except Alice's university misfortune, and half expected a slap across the face, so he was surprised by her muffled giggles sneaking out from behind her covered her mouth.

"I can just imagine poor Alice's face as she read them. She must have died of embarrassment. Just think if she'd remembered to cancel the paper, you'd have got away with it."

"So you can see how she only wants to be friends from now on. And even that's been put in jeopardy by my ex."

"What's happened to the egocentric Theo? I didn't take you for some-one who cared so deeply about others."

"People change. I haven't got time to hang around, and she may need longer than I anticipate."

"What's the rush, Casanova? Give the poor woman time; she can't fail to succumb to your charms again eventually."

He did not want to tell her everything. He could not risk Alice find-ing out. She put down her empty glass and stared at him before he moved to sit at the table in the kitchen. The next thing he heard was his front door closing softly.

Alice heard a key in her front door and held her breath, listening out for one or two sets of footsteps. When she only heard high heels she crawled out of bed and slipped on her dressing gown.

"God, sorry, did I wake you? How's your head?" Zoe asked, slipping off her shoes.

"I wasn't asleep. How was your evening?"

"Pleasant and informative. You didn't tell me about Theo being a journalist, you bad girl. However, it made me roar with laughter."

"Well I'm glad you felt that way. Personally, I felt violated." Alice moved to the fridge and poured herself a glass of cold milk. "I didn't expect you home so early, if at all, if I'm honest."

"Theo and I don't have much in common. He's far too old for me, really. Anyway, I'm going to bed. I'll catch an earlier train tomorrow so I'll be out of your hair."

She was disappointed by Zoe's lack of information. She wanted to hear more about Theo. How he was keeping, did he still look tired and haunted, did he mention her?

Alice was awoken by a stream of sunshine breaking through a chink in the curtains. It was later than usual. She had not intended to lie in so long, but a fractious night's sleep had left her feeling drained.

She padded into the kitchen and found Zoe putting a mug in the sink.

"Have you had breakfast?"

"I've had a coffee, I'll grab something on the train. Thanks so much for offering your flat as a crash-pad. Next time I come down let's make sure you can come out too." She leant in and pecked Alice on the cheek. "And by the way, Theo was disappointed you couldn't come out last night. Be nice to him, I think he misses you."

There was no time for her to glean more information from Zoe as the taxi driver rang the buzzer. Alice waved her off, wondering what Theo had said for Zoe to think he misses her.

Theo had a fractious night's sleep, thanks to a grinding headache gnawing at his brain. When the phone rang, the shrill sound bore into his temples, making him wince. Picking up the receiver, he heard Joanna's grating voice.

"I got a phone call from Justin late last night saying he was okay but he's never coming home, and he doesn't want any contact with us for the foreseeable future. You know what that means, don't you?"

"It means I may not see my son before I die."

"No, it means I'll be all alone when you die. I'll have to fend for myself."

"For God's sake, Joanna, not everything revolves around you. And what do you want me to do about it?"

"I want you to be understanding and supportive, like . . ."

"Like when we were married?" he interjected. "I think we have very different memories of those years. Perhaps you should persuade Rory to come back, seeing as the reason for his departure has vanished."

She went quiet, with only the sound of her breathing letting him know she was still there. He waited before speaking again.

"We made unwise decisions in the past so let's not travel down that road again. I'm sorry about Justin and Rory, but I'm no longer obligated to tend to your needs." And with that he hung up.

With the low rumblings of a headache pressing in the background, he mulled over his predicament with Alice. Was Zoe right? Was he actually in love with her? Not that it mattered, he reminded himself, it was too late to do anything about it now.

Chapter 32

Sitting on the bus enabled Alice to glimpse into the lives of other people as she stared into their front rooms. Many windows displayed a large Christmas tree adorned with multi-coloured baubles and twinkling fairy lights.

She imagined the fun involved in decorating the tree with a loved one and children, their wide eyes drinking in all the twinkling drama.

The fripperies of the festive season only highlighted her pain and loneliness at the most excruciating time of the year, so she had refrained from partaking in purchasing anything remotely festive.

The hospice, however, was decorated tastefully. White Christmas lights were strung up outside the building, and fairy lights were wrapped around the standard box trees either side of the front door.

Inside, angels were a repetitive theme running from room to room, and Alice took some comfort in them. A large tree, reaching the ceiling, was placed in the dining room, and Christmas cards hung on long pieces string like clothes on a washing line. Gentle chorale music played in the reception area.

The hospice suited Alice well, and Sadie had noticed the guests enjoyed her company.

"How are you holding up?" asked Sadie.

"Fine thanks."

"As long as being here isn't detrimental to your own wellbeing." She placed her hand on Alice's shoulder. "Some of us are going for a Christmas drink tomorrow evening. You're welcome to join us."

"Thanks, I'll bear that in mind."

She hadn't lied, she felt needed in the hospice, and the invitation made her feel good, but she knew the tears would spill over later in the solitude of her flat as she accepted the fact that her newly acquired social anxiety was gaining new grounds, forcing her to remain cocooned in the four walls of her flat.

A nurse came up to Alice and asked her if she could read to a guest. She was glad for the distraction.

The woman looked a picture of perfection in her pure white dressing gown and matching cashmere bed socks. Her hair shone with silvery-grey flecks.

"I've been looking forward to meeting you; I've heard many good things about you. Come sit with me," she said, patting the chair next to her.

Alice sat down and smelt a delicious mélange of rose and juniper surrounding her like a colourful aura, repelling the negative arrows aiming at her own mind.

"Now dear, who or what gives your life special meaning?"

Alice blushed, searching for an answer on the floor. "I don't have a special person in my life."

"I don't understand how someone like you is single. It's a pity you won't meet anyone here, dear," she smiled.

Alice shrugged, picking up a book from the table in front of them. "Is this the book you want me to read?"

"I can read just fine. I just wanted some company; I get lonely sometimes."

"I'm sorry. Would you like me to find some activity for you in the day room?"

"I haven't the energy for that. Talking will suit me." She paused to cough. "You shouldn't surround yourself with illness too much. Let some love flow into your heart. I did once and it was the most beautiful experience of my life."

"What happened?"

"We were married for forty-two glorious years. We had two children and a home full of joy and love. We didn't have much money but that didn't seem to matter." She smiled, closing her eyes briefly. "He sadly died last year, but that doesn't take away the years of happiness we had, and the memories we made."

"You must miss him terribly."

"I do, but he told me he'd be waiting for me on God's front lawn, so I take comfort in that."

"I've never heard it described like that. The imagery is beautiful."

Joan smiled as dark circles drifted under her eyes. Her eyelids began to dip, and silence reigned as a faint smile whispered on her lips. Alice sat with her for a while, noticing the peace enveloping the room. She placed a blanket over her knees before leaving quietly.

Joan's words washed around Alice's mind, as images of Theo came to the foreground. She had not heard from him since that inauspicious evening, allowing her heart to finally begin healing.

Christmas Eve arrived as though her life had hit the fast forward button. The icy pavements were cluttered with people, crushing one another with bulging bags, and spikes of wrapping paper protruding upwards, as though jousting for position on the pavement.

A cluster of people from the local church had assembled on the street corner, singing carols and collecting money for charity. The smell of mulled wine coated the air, and a chill nipped at the tips of exposed ears and fingers.

Alice dodged people as she hurried home with a bag of shopping clutched tightly to her chest. She felt invisible amongst the chattering families, and husbands frantically looking for last minute gifts for their wives. Father Christmas would not be visiting her that night, she thought wryly, so she relented and bought herself a scented candle, a bottle of Asti, and a large box of Thornton's chocolates. There were plenty of good things to watch on TV, so the evening would pass quickly, and tomorrow was just another day in her monotonous week.

The warm air of her flat caressed her chilled face as she hung up her heavy tweed coat and woolly hat. Modern Christmas songs pounded through the wall, so she switched on her radio to help screen them out.

Looking down at the streets below, she wondered whether Theo was preparing a round of festive social events, involving an array of stunning women. It saddened her to think the connection they once had was nothing but a farce, leaving her with nothing tangible to hold onto except for some newspaper cuttings mocking the whole event.

The street lights glowered in the early evening gloom, and a shower of rain peppered the pavement below, turning it to tarnished copper.

The neighbour's music finally stopped, allowing her to relax. Closing her eyes, she pictured her mother baking mince pies before her illness damaged her, and suddenly she felt less lonely.

Theo contemplated calling Joanna to see if she had heard from Justin, but he felt too weak to deal with her ascorbic attitude. So he remained in his seat with Rufus curled up on his knee, and a glass of mulled wine in his hand.

He had come to realize, over the past few months, that Alice had offered him more than any other woman he had ever known. Her physique may not have been the most appealing he had ever caressed, but she was accepting of his unappealing quirks and open to forgiving him his errors, unlike Joanna.

He took his mobile out of his pocket and sent a Christmas wishes text to Justin. As it disappeared into the ether he wondered whether Justin would read it or even receive it. It seemed a lonely time of year for his son to choose to be on his own, and he hoped Joanna would have the opportunity to welcome him back to the diminishing family circle in the near future.

He was flicking through his contacts on his mobile when he came across Alice's number. His thumb hovered over the button to call her. He paused. A bead of sweat trickled down his temple before he put the mobile on the table and picked up his drink. He emptied the glass before topping it up then tipping a couple of tablets into his mouth.

Waking up in his chair a few hours later, the dull ache had dissipated, and the nausea had gone. It surprised him how sleeping during the day refreshed him, yet paradoxically made him feel like an old man.

The sound of people chatting outside intrigued him, and for a brief moment he thought they were heading his way. Curiosity drew him to the bay window, where he saw the group wrapped up in coats glistening with raindrops. They held bottles of wine and gifts wrapped up in silver paper, decorated with red ribbons and bows. They headed into his neighbour's house.

He reminisced back to his time as a rookie journalist, when office parties were du rigueur, and he and Joanna would host their own parties in their early days. Even when their relationship was teetering on the edge of destruction, Joanna would still hold fabulous parties at Christmas. He was surrounded by food, drink, and people eager to entertain him, whether he wanted it or not. The latter gained strength as their marriage progressed.

He imagined Joanna would still have friends whom she could call upon. She would never be lonely, unlike himself. He now had the company of a dozen books he needed to review, although he had a feeling he would not get the time to read and review them all. His body kept cutting out on him, as though he had some faulty wiring hidden amongst his vast nervous system.

He desperately wanted to tell Alice about his health to ease the burden from his shoulders, and for her to hold him and tell him all would be okay, even though he knew it wouldn't be.

Chapter 33

"Did you have a good Christmas Day?" Sadie asked, as Alice entered the day room.

Alice smiled a smile which conveyed a modicum of sadness to those who cared to look closely. Sadie noticed as she always did. Alice enquired about Sadie's Christmas, as her sisters were over from Jamaica.

"Don't feel obliged to come in over this festive period. Families usually visit at least once."

"I'd rather keep myself busy. It's my first Christmas without my mother."

Sadie was about to speak when she was distracted by the arrival of another family bearing gifts. She excused herself before bustling over to them.

Alice observed families huddled together, sharing some of the last drops of life with their loved ones. Hands offering the comfort of touch, reaching out to the almost angels, bringing solace and understanding without the need for words, whilst laughter, smiles, and reminiscing bounced of every wall. She found solace in those moments as they went some way to soothe the entangled clump of emotional anguish in her heart. She thought she was healing, but she was fooling herself and she knew it.

A frail hand reached up and touched hers. "I'd like to go back to my room, please," said Connie, her almost transparent face looking up at her.

Alice pushed Connie back to her room and gently eased her out of the wheelchair, back into her bed.

"Somebody loves you and needs you," whispered Connie as Alice tucked her in.

"That's sweet of you to say, but I doubt it."

"I can sense someone is thinking of you. I was a psychic when I was younger. I still have the gift, you know."

Alice smiled into her toffee coloured eyes, not believing, but not wishing to be rude.

She sat down on the chair next to Connie's bed and picked up a book of poetry from the bedside table. She read a poem from the page where the book fell open. A smile drifted gently across Connie's lips as she mouthed along with the words.

When Connie fell into a peaceful slumber, Alice replaced the book and stepped quietly out of the bedroom.

Theo had refused to attend any of the invitations he had received over the Christmas period, and he was doubly pleased with his decision since his blurred vision and poor balance was hampering his mobility. He also found his headaches worsened if he bent down, coughed, or sneezed.

He had ensconced himself in his leather chair and surrounded himself with his medication, alcohol, books, snacks, and the TV remote. He had made sure he did not need to move for the next few hours.

However, he began feeling lonely. After separating from Joanna he usually had a girlfriend to stay over for Christmas to fulfil his every need. He was used to being adored and entertained. Even Rufus had abandoned his lap for his basket.

His mind wandered in the direction of Joanna, and he wondered what his life would have been like had he not strayed. Perhaps he would have become immune to her nagging over the years, or perhaps she would have become more passive. He laughed at the preposterous thought, and the laugh echoed around the room, underlining the emptiness around him.

He kept checking his mobile but it remained obstinately quiet, and his contentment levels dipped further as the day progressed.

The bus jolted as it sped Alice home. She wanted to stay on at the hospice, but Sadie insisted she return home, as she herself was also doing.

Alice did not have the courage to refuse, so she found herself on the bus, looking at her solitary reflection in the window.

The sound of bass thudded through the wall as she entered her flat. The three Christmas cards she had received from Sadie, Zoe, and Maggie and Marcus, sat on the windowsill next to a wilting azalea, and a photo of her mother when she was a young woman. She felt Maggie and Marcus would have sent a card to everyone who attended their retreat purely in the hopes of attracting their custom again.

She received periodic e-mails from Zoe, who was buzzing about working with an editor on her book. She was due to stay with Alice at the time of her book release in May, so she could attend book signings. Alice dreaded the invasion of her small space again, but could not find a way to express that to Zoe. She blamed her mother for her affability, blushing as she did so.

Another date loomed ominously over Alice's shoulder, that of New Year's Eve. Since her mother's illness, New Year's Eve had been a quiet affair. They would have a meal in the kitchen before watching the celebrations, including the chimes of Big Ben, on the TV. It suited them both to be on the outside looking in.

It was not always like that. For her short period of time at university, Alice sampled the party life, enjoying a frenzy of socializing with other students. She was undecided whether it was worse having known what life could be like, or whether it would have been kinder to have never known what existed beyond the foyer door.

Music boomed through the wall from the neighbour. She sighed. Noise was not conducive to writing, and writing was all she had left in her life. She packed her notebook and pen in her handbag and set off for the local café.

There were two women with weather-bedraggled hair sitting at a table when she arrived. The table next to the window, which was partially steamed up with condensation, was vacant, so she took a seat and ordered a cappuccino and a mince pie. Removing the leather-bound notebook and pink pen from her bag, she stroked the cover before placing them on the table.

Ideas trickled into her mind which she scribbled down, painfully aware that not one of them was blessed with an all-important hook. Taking a nibble of the mince pie, she looked up to see Theo staring at her through the window. Dusting crumbs from around her mouth, she offered him a faint smile.

The bell jingled as he stepped inside.

"I was just coming to see you," he said, removing his hat.

"Really? Well lucky you found me here then."

"May I?" he said, pointing to the chair.

Once seated he ordered a coffee.

"What were you coming to see me about?" she asked, picking up her cup.

"I'm not sure really, I just felt I should see you."

"'Felt' you should see me?" she snipped, replacing the cup in the saucer rather clumsily.

"Perhaps that wasn't the right way to put it. What I meant to say was I wanted to come and see you."

Alice felt her cheeks prickly with heat. Then noticing her open notebook, she hurriedly closed it.

"Am I disturbing your writing?"

"My neighbours are really noisy, so I thought I'd try writing here."

"Is it working out?"

"Not really, I still get distracted. I think I've got my protagonist right, I just don't always like her."

"No one is totally likeable in real life, Alice. The reader needs believable characters, not some adult version of Cinderella."

His analogy made her laugh, and the sound surprised her; how long was it since she had last laughed? That's right, it was in France. "The best writing I did was in France; in fact it was the best time of my life."

"Really," he replied, tentatively putting his hand on top of hers.

She felt his touch travel through his fingertips, and memories of

France exploded in her mind. She was transported back to the intimate times they shared, raising the hairs on the back of her neck. She exhaled loudly before pulling her hand away.

"You've hurt me deeply; I can't seem to move passed the incident with your ex."

"I'm sorry I didn't do more to defend you; Joanna has a negative effect on me."

"A poor excuse." Her eyes tightened.

"You're still young and attractive, get out there and find someone who'd be good for you."

Alice laughed. "You don't believe that. You're still teasing me to this day."

She drained the cup and pushed the half-eaten mince pie to one side, before pulling on her coat. "I wish you well, Theo, but I'm not going to play your games. Please don't contact me or seek me out anymore." And with that she bolted.

Over the following few days, Theo's health took a rapid decline. His headaches increased in intensity, and his mobility became highly impaired. When his neighbour found him collapsed at his front door an ambulance was called.

The doctor in the hospital spent some time with him, checking his ideas for his care had not changed; ensuring palliative care was his intended option.

New Year's Eve promised to be as uneventful as when her mother was alive. Alice opened her fridge and noted the contents: skimmed milk, low-fat spread, cheese, two red peppers, and a large block of chocolate. Hardly the fridge of a party girl, she mused.

She flicked through the TV guide and saw the poor choice of scheduled programmes. That decided it for her, she was going to contact Sadie and ask to volunteer; she needed to be needed.

"We do have a full house and not enough volunteers, so your help would be much appreciated."

"I hope you are feeling comfortable, Theo," asked Sadie.

"Very, thank you," he replied in a hoarse rasp.

"Push this button when you want another dose of pain relief," she said, pointing to the self-giving infusion set by his hand. She noted the mottling of his extremities and the emptiness in his eyes. She had seen it so many times before; she knew what was coming.

Theo blinked slowly and felt the button with his fingertips. He could see the end in sight, and he couldn't get there quick enough.

Stepping onto the bus, Alice found a seat behind a pair of young lovers practicing their midnight kiss. She smiled at their joy, whilst her heart cramped.

One minute the bus was cruising along the darkening street and the next the brakes were screeching eerily, thrusting passengers first forward then back hard in their seats.

The couple in front of Alice whipped out their mobile phones and began filming the carnage outside. Clasping her hand against her chest, she craned to see what was going on, and saw a car with smoke rising from the crumpled bonnet, and a body slumped over the steering wheel.

"Is he dead?" squealed a girl, gawking through the window.

Her words caused a frantic stir amongst the passengers. The windows were steamed up, forcing people to rub the glass with their gloved hands and peer through the blurry patches.

Suddenly, the inside of the bus was illuminated with flashing blue lights and the piercing sound of sirens. Alice noted the bus driver talking to a policeman through his window, before standing up and announcing that they were all to find an alternative way to continue their journey, as the road ahead would be closed for hours.

Her heart sank as images of the people at the hospice awaiting her arrival floated before her eyes. She didn't want to disappoint them. Standing up, she shuffled along the bus with the other passengers, jostling with over-sized handbags and bulky winter coats.

Cold air blasted her face as she alighted. Turning her collar up, she headed for the underground along with most of the other passengers, their heads bowed down against the buffering wind.

The tube rattled through the tunnels, speeding Alice in the direction of the hospice, although she was not sure how to actually get there from the station. She was standing, squashed against a man's armpit with an umbrella prodding her in her back. But the discomfort did nothing to assuage her anxiety at being in an over-crowded space.

Her ruminations turned towards Theo who had offered her a half-hearted apology, which she sensed he only did to coerce her back into bed, to then mock her again.

Once she reached the pavement outside, she pulled away from the crowd and stopped to orientate herself. She was unfamiliar with the area, and the darkness did not help.

Rain fell, covering her hair in fine droplets, making it frizzy. She ploughed along the street, zigzagging her way through revellers who had already begun their alcoholic journey towards the new year.

Her shoulders relaxed at the sight of the twinkling white lights at the front of the hospice. Stepping inside, she shook her head like a shaggy dog, sending tiny droplets cascading over her shoulders.

Sadie greeted her with her trademark wide smile, placing both her hands on Alice's shoulders. "So glad you could make it, we're rather stretched. I wonder if you could help Phyllis in the dayroom, she's trying to get people settled to watch the show and Big Ben later."

Alice found the dayroom to be a hive of activity, with the guests and their families gathered together.

Her eyes were drawn to a couple in their thirties sitting at a table by a window. They were lost in each other's gaze and holding hands across the table. The woman had a scarlet and gold headscarf wrapped around her head, matching the off-the-shoulder scarlet dress she was wearing. Her collar bone protruded sharply like the cheekbones on her face.

A tap on her elbow jolted Alice, and turning she found Connie standing there.

"Now why is a beautiful young lady hanging around here on such an auspicious evening, instead of attending a swanky party?"

"I don't think swanky parties exist for people like me. For you in your day, perhaps."

"Oh yes," she replied wistfully, "I attended many parties to start the new year off with a bang. Memories are all I have now."

Alice threaded Connie's arm through hers and led her to a table of women, and after introductions left Connie to enjoy the evening as much as possible. New Year's Eve was usually synonymous with hope and dreams for the future, but in the hospice, for many it welcomed in the year they knew they may die.

"Alice, I hate to put upon you, but I wonder if you'd sit with a guest. He's not looking well and I think he'd appreciate some quiet company. He's in room four," Sadie requested.

Alice moved silently down the corridor and knocked on the bedroom door. When she heard no reply, she opened it slowly, peering round into the dimly lit room. She saw a man lying in bed propped up with several pillows with a self-giving set attached to his arm. He was facing the window seemingly looking at the stars pressed into the velvety sky.

She did not want to startle him so she coughed gently. As his head turned towards her, she noticed how the gentle light caught his tired yet enquiring eyes.

"Theo?" she said, stepping closer to the bed. She noticed he had lost weight since the last time they met.

"What are you doing here?" he asked hoarsely.

"I'm a volunteer. I never expected to see you here."

"The prerequisite is to be close to death, or so I understand," he whispered with a wry smile.

Alice felt a lump in her throat threaten to rise. "Why didn't you tell me you were ill? I mean, did you know you were ill when we last met?"

"I didn't think you'd care." He paused, his forehead crumpling as he waited for the pain to pass.

Alice blinked frantically. "Can I do something for you?"

"Only death will give me the peace I'm looking for now. You can't give me that, can you?"

"Oh Theo." She felt a tear streak her cheek.

"I'm upsetting you again, I'm sorry," he rasped.

"It's not your fault this time."

"Maybe not, but I'm sure many people will say I'm getting what I deserve."

"Nonsense, you didn't murder anyone, you just highlighted people's deficiencies and foibles for others to laugh at. You were cruel but you don't deserve this."

"Your generosity of heart is astounding. You of all people could rejoice in my suffering, and I wouldn't blame you if you did."

"After our time together in France, I could never hate you. I'm hurt you think that."

"Sorry."

She smiled softly. "Rest now, I'll stay by your side. Would you like me to read something to you?"

Theo shook his head slowly from side to side.

Alice found herself holding her breath as she watched his chest rise and fall. She touched the backs of his hands and parted the salt-and-pepper hairs.

Theo inhaled deeply, murmuring as he jolted awake.

"It's fortuitous we meet again in these last moments," he said, before wetting his encrusted lips with his tongue. "During our absence from one another I came to realize I'd fallen in love with you. But by the time I knew that I was already diagnosed, so I knew I'd left it too late." He screwed his eyes shut, placing his hand lightly on top of hers. "I want you to finish your novel and follow your dream. Don't let people like me put you off."

"I'm doing my best, but the words aren't flowing at the moment."

"Perhaps after this is over you'll rediscover the joy and passion of writing."

Alice smiled, but was not sure he saw it in the gloom. He squeezed her hand and beckoned her to come closer.

"I love you, Alice Calwin. We'll always have France."

Alice clamped her lips together, shuffling closer so she could touch his cheek with the tip of her nose and nuzzle him like a puppy. He turned his head slowly and planted a kiss on her forehead.

"Perhaps we'll meet again."

She was about to reply when she felt his head dip heavily onto her. She sat up carefully and touched his face with the pads of her fingers. Nothing. She moved her hand to his chest and pressed down hoping to feel the rise and fall of his steady breathing.

Alice laid her head on his chest, allowing the tears to run over the bridge of her nose and settle in a damp patch on his pyjama top.

Quietly, she got up and opened the window before heading off to find a nurse.

Chapter 34

It was only six o'clock in the morning, but Alice was already at her desk writing the denouement of her novel. She looked out to see the sky blushing as the sun rose, stretching its fingers and caressing the curves of the land. Birds sitting on apple-blossom-laden branches ushered the day in with their chorus, whilst clumps of daffodils stood erect with their yellow-tipped buds and green fronds.

Rufus sauntered into the room and leapt onto her lap, prodding her thighs for a few seconds before curling up and resting his head on her knee. She stroked him along his spine, surprised how well he had taken to her; it made sharing the home easier.

After Theo's death, she was contacted by his solicitor to find she was the recipient of his house and cat. There was also a substantial amount of money for her, even after a large portion had been left to Justin.

She worked through her depressive state and gave up her job in the bakery to concentrate on writing, whilst continuing to volunteer at the hospice; it had become an integral part of her life.

Maggie bustled around the patio serving refreshing drinks to the group who were sheltering from the heat under parasols. Enid and Doris fanned themselves with folded pieces of paper, and Zoe cooled herself by pressing a chilled bottle of water against her neck. Alice stood on the edge of the patio, gazing towards the olive grove.

"It's wonderful to see you again," gushed Maggie as she sidled up to Alice. "I'm sorry it's under these circumstances though."

"Being here is like being with Theo again. I thought it meant nothing to him but I was wrong."

Maggie put her arm around her shoulders. "It's a beautiful thing to do, and Marcus and I are honoured you want to do it here."

"I think this was the last place he was happy, I know it was for me."

Maggie gave her a squeeze.

"It's right to have everyone here, even Clive. We were all a part of the charade, and we all need to say goodbye."

The pair turned to see Clive walk over to the table where Enid and Doris sat. After a few words he kissed both of their hands and sat down. Zoe was leaning against the chateaux wall talking to a young man.

"That's Enzo, a local we've hired to help around the place. He seems to be getting on well with Zoe," laughed Maggie.

"He looks a little young for her."

"I think she may actually like that."

The two women giggled quietly before walking back to the table where the others were seated. Alice sat down with them.

"Oh my dear, you've lost weight. You haven't been looking after yourself, have you?" quizzed Doris, frowning.

"I've been through a rough patch, but this will bring me some form of closure."

"We're all here for you," said Clive, reaching out tentatively before withdrawing his hand swiftly.

Alice closed her eyes and listened to the blissful silence, pierced only by the guttural sound of the cicadas. A warm breeze caressed the back of her neck, feeling like Theo's hand was touching her. She closed her eyes to be with him. *I miss you.*

Alice retired to the bedroom she once shared with Theo, and walked out onto the balcony to enjoy the cooler evening air. Below, Clive, Maggie, and Marcus were sitting around a table, engrossed in conversation. Marcus's legs were stretched out like a lounging flamingo.

The smell of cigarette smoke snagged in her nostrils. She searched around and saw Zoe standing with Enzo, smoking. She watched him pass his cigarette over, for her to inhale slowly before blowing the smoke skywards, then handing it back to him. She remembered Theo offering her a cigarette and how she coughed instead of looking sexy like Zoe looked. She regretted that.

She returned inside, half expecting to see Theo stretched out across the bed, cradling his head in his hands as he used to do. The empty bed stabbed her in the heart, and emptied her lungs of breath like a punch to the stomach.

A reverend hush filled the dining room as Alice entered; murmurings of greetings sparked across the room like the synapse firing across the brain. A gentle smile and nod was all that was needed from her. There was no need for words at that time. She sought out the table she often shared with Theo, which the others had thoughtfully left vacant.

Maggie brought her coffee and a croissant. "Try and eat a little bit," she urged.

Alice broke off one end and dunked it in her coffee before popping it in her mouth. She still half expected Theo to stride into the room and pull out a chair at her table, bringing with him the pungent aroma of Gauloises. She finished her coffee before returning to her room as quietly as she had arrived.

The urn with Theo's ashes stood on the bedside table. Picking it up, she pressed it into her chest and imagined she could feel his heartbeat. She held it so tightly her arms ached.

When she returned downstairs, still clutching the urn, she found the rest of the group, including Maggie and Marcus, standing around in the hall. They all filed out behind her in silence and followed her towards the olive trees.

She paused in front of the tree where Marlon hanged himself. They all stood in a semi-circle and Clive uttered words of apology, his voice trembling with every word. He then stepped forward and placed a single rose at the base of the tree.

The procession then moved to a tree on the edge of the land which overlooked a panoramic vista. Alice gave the urn one last squeeze whilst trying to utter a few words. Her wide eyes caught Zoe's, who stepped forward, turning to face the group.

"None of us knew Theo as much as Alice did, but we all had a connection with him during the retreat. I must say when I discovered he was actually a journalist I had to laugh. I laughed even harder when I finally found his thoughts on us; he'd understood my flaws perfectly." She paused to smile, looking in Alice's direction. "I remember watching him with Alice with a touch of envy; they had a connection I hope to find with someone special, eventually." She stepped back a pace.

Inhaling deeply, Alice twisted the lid off the urn and spoke softly to the contents as though they were particles of Theo's soul, rather than dust-like matter. She slowly tipped the contents of the urn around the base of an olive tree, watching the motes twist and flutter in the sunlight. As the last ashes fell upon the ground, she allowed her lungs to release the stale, grieving air before inhaling a fresh breath.

Zoe moved forward and linked arms with her for the slow stroll back to the chateaux, where Enzo had prepared drinks.

Alice gazed wistfully at the clear turquoise sky until she felt a hand on her elbow. She turned to see Doris smiling up at her.

"You still have precious memories of him; they won't fade." She patted Alice on the arm in a motherly gesture.

As Doris moved away, Clive sidled up to Alice and coughed.

"Do you think everyone will eventually forgive me for what happened to Marlon?"

"I'm sure no one holds you totally responsible, you may have had a part to play but you didn't place the noose around his neck."

"Succinctly put. It's a shame there's still a stigma attached to being gay in some people's eyes," he sighed.

"Perhaps it stemmed from his family's attitude. None of us really knew Marlon or where he came from."

"Families have a lot to answer for."

"Is that said from personal experience?"

"Let's just say, I had the crap beaten out of me weekly by my father and older brother, but I remained gay, much to their disgust."

Alice placed her hand on his, tapping it a couple of times. "Shall we have a drink and toast the memories of the two men?"

"Why not."

A year later, Alice sat in the airy bedroom in the chateaux with a glass of wine on the desk next to her laptop.

She was on the final edit of her novel, *A Love That Never Was*, due to be published just before Christmas.

She stood up to stretch her legs, and wandered to the window. The white muslin curtains fluttered in the breeze, allowing her to see the tables below occupied by holiday makers, keeping Maggie and Marcus's dream alive.

Alice smiled as she sensed Theo standing behind her.

I love you too, Theo. Until we meet again on God's front lawn.

Acknowledgments

I want to thank Jessica "Goose" Kristie and James Koukis at Winter Goose Publishing for their continued support and faith in me.

About the Author

Hemmie Martin spent most of her professional life as a Community Nurse for people with learning disabilities, a Family Planning Nurse, and a Forensic Nurse working with young offenders. She spent six years living in the south of France, and currently lives in Essex with her husband, a house rabbit, and a guinea pig. Her eldest daughter, Jessica, is studying veterinary medicine, and her other daughter is doing a degree in Computer Science.

Follow Hemmie on her website, Facebook & Twitter.